One or Several Deserts

Copyright © 2023 Carter St. Hogan
All rights reserved

This book may not be reproduced in whole or in part, except for the inclusion of brief quotations in a review, without permission in writing from the author or publisher. No part of this publication may be reproduced, stored in or introduced into a retrieval system, or transmitted, in any form, or by any means (electronic, mechanical, photocopying, recording, or otherwise), without prior permission of the publisher.

Requests for permission should be directed to 1111@1111press.com, or mailed to 11:11 Press LLC, 4732 13th Ave S, Minneapolis, MN 55407.

Design by Mike Corrao
Cover Art by Asher Ford (Object Lover) and Carter St. Hogan

Paperback: 9781948687607

Printed in the United States of America

FIRST AMERICAN EDITION

9 8 7 6 5 4 3 2 1

A startling debut full of stories that refuse to be polite and that challenge what you thought you knew about genre, about fiction, and even about prose itself. Carter St. Hogan puts the magic back into magical realism and then cracks it back open and turns it inside out and leaves its glorious insides streaming in the wind of their words. Transgressive, sacrilegious, touching on a unique and previously unknown fleshy gnosticism: this is a roadmap for where the fantastic has yet to go.

– Brian Evenson

One or Several Deserts by Carter St. Hogan unlocks, transfigures, and destroys. This book of short stories pushed me towards a new knowledge unlocked through seeing the body as it is; cut open & bloodlet. Each story builds, breaks, and bleeds all over the reader, an argument for survival in a violent world. Carter St Hogan proves that writing is nourishment towards our collective continuing.

– LA Warman

Carter St. Hogan's fearlessly innovative, unsettling stories run amok with a stark tenderness, and whirlwind poetic prose, that their fabric often lingers like only the best writing can. A not-to-miss, startling debut.

– Fernando A. Flores

The way Carter's language spiders through these stories does a
certain thing to my brain—akin to napping in a bed of knives.
Tuck yourself in.

– John Elizabeth Stinzi

One or Several Deserts is the debut of an extraordinarily gifted
writer who manages both surface and depth in ways few others even try. Here is some of the most dazzling prose I have
read in quite some time. With this collection, Carter St. Hogan
emerges as a literary artist of significant originality and accom-
plishment.

– Garielle Lutz

ONE OR SEVERAL DESERTS

CARTER ST. HOGAN

TABLE OF CONTENTS

I am the beast at the end of the rope.

— Sarah Kane, *Crave*

PIG

Pigs can't skin themselves. My husband says this to my son every morning over cereal. He says it to me also, but when he says it to me it's because he's being a *jackass*. This is an English word I learned recently from the pigs.

The pigs agree with my jackass husband. "You can't hold a knife without opposable thumbs," they grumble at each other. "And anyway, it would be a violation to do our own skinning. You wouldn't embalm yourself, would you, New Wife?"

"I might," I tell them.

When my husband first drove my son and me in his pickup truck from the airport to his confinement, I knew there must be pigs somewhere, but I couldn't see them. Low metal buildings nested in rows a dozen deep. My husband pointed at a lake a few miles away.

"Lagoon," he said. "No. Not ever."

My husband's favorite thing about me is that I am not good with English.

He took us through all the buildings, his chest puffed out, his face scruff barely concealing his grin. I couldn't see what he was so proud of. There were hundreds of pink pigs in each of the metal buildings, crammed into pens so tightly they couldn't move. Two males in what I now know to be the fattening pen screamed and ripped savagely at each other's hides. In one building, there were crates of pregnant mothers too round to stand. In another, blind, staggering piglets bleated weakly as men in rubber suits clipped their ears and tails.

My son, a lover of pigs, giggled.

"Their faces bleed," he laughed in Hungarian, his eyes full of their bared teeth.

"Enough," I would have said, had I known the English word.

My father was a pig farmer all his life. Before him, his father was a pig farmer. Before him, his father was a pig farmer. Before him, his father was briefly a jeweler for Austro-Hungarian aristocrats, and then he became a pig farmer. My husband is a pig farmer. One day, my son will become a pig farmer.

My father's pig farm was a wooden hut and a beech forest where furry pigs ran free over the roots of white trees. Hungarian pigs are not the bristly, immobile masses my husband raises. Mangalitsa is their real name, though my son called them "woolies." They could be mistaken for sheep, they have such thick, curly hair. The sound they make when they snuffle in the snow is like the kindest sort of laughter. I loved to run my hand through their black and creamy curls and then smell their musky oil in my skin. They are good, wild pigs, and my son rode them like horses and slept with them in the forest until the first snows of the season, when I made him come to the hearth. On winter mornings, my father shoveled a path through the snow to the house of the pigs so I could bring them warmed water and our steaming dinner slop. Their grunts echoed against the vast, crispy ice. "Thank you, Moon Face," they called to me. The white walls rose beside me, the stars glittered down, the mountains crumpled like old leather faces.

My husband's pig farm isn't even called a farm. Nevertheless, he works with pigs, however bristly and immobile, and this is why I married him. Love has nothing to do with it; he simply put his hands to my nose so I could smell the pig on his skin, and then he offered me two visas. My son, my new husband and I were on a plane within hours.

"Make for me a grand soap bowl tonight," my husband said to me on my first night.

"Make what?" I asked. My son blinked up, uncomprehending. My son had no understanding of English beyond the words "pig" and "leaving."

"A grand soap bowl," my husband repeated, angry. My

husband is American and not fond of repeating himself. "I will be cold from the [word I didn't know], and I will like some soap."

"Yes, all right," I answered.

While my husband toiled in the cold of the word I didn't know, my son and I made a grand soap bowl. All afternoon it took us. I had smuggled with me a small box of *salo*, made from my father's pigs, and I carved the oxidized fat from the upper paprika-orange layers, which my son scooped into a large pot. I boiled and rendered and strained, then emptied the white puffy stinking fat into a large silver bowl. When the soap was hard, I gave my son and myself each two metal spoons and we set to carving out the bowl.

When we neared completion, my husband arrived home at dusk. He stared down at us where we sat at his kitchen table. My sleeves were rolled past my elbows, my son's hair curled with sweat, and the kitchen was coated in the thick smell of pig soap.

"Where is my soap?" he demanded.

I held up the silver bowl. "Right here, husband."

My husband tightened his fist. My son stared.

"Where is my soap?" he said again, slowly.

"Soap?" I asked, hesitant.

"S-o-u-p," spelled my husband. "Soup."

"My English," I pleaded.

My husband erupted in laughter. It hurtled out of his muddy, smeared body. He clutched the edge of the table to keep himself upright. My son flinched and held his spoon out in front of him, as if warding away evil.

"Oh, poor wife," my husband laughed. "You are too stupid for your own good."

"I…sorry?" I tried, unsure now if even that was the appropriate phrase at this time.

"Yes," he agreed, patting my head like a child, "I know you are." He looked at my son. "Isn't dumb mommy very, very sorry?"

"Soup," my son said quietly in English.

"Look!" cried my jackass husband. "Even your five-year old son can say the right word!"

"You're just here to slum it with us," say the pigs in the third fattening pen. They're wrong. I like the way they sound. The words they use. The pigs in the fattening pen are crude, and I like the way they curse each other with names like "crackle" and "chop," "hock" and "rind," as though they're preparing their minds for the divisions of their bodies after they go to slaughter. I like that they can understand me. Pigs always do.

"You can't just come into our pen and act like you belong here," the pigs say.

"Let me stay," I beg.

"There isn't room," says a pig whose ear has been bitten off. He has long scars running all across his body. The other pigs like to pick on him. Now he picks on me. There is a clump of fecal matter smeared on his nose.

"Go bother the mothers," says the pig who clicks his teeth. "They're always talking."

The pigs snort together in agreement. Then the pig with one ear knocks into the pig who does all the biting, and they snarl at each other. Just in time, I step lightly past the flushed bodies and out through the cage door. The fight is so loud I can hear it rattle the tin siding.

My husband does not abide by my son's "peasant upbringing." He clips my son's hair and keeps him in clean shirts with small, embroidered men riding horses on the lapel. When my son is allowed to see the pigs, it is on an arranged occasion, and my husband is the one to take him. He leads my wild boy through the aisles of contained animals. He doesn't like me being in the confinement, but he can't legally stop me, and I refuse to stay in the house on the hill.

When I am inside the confinement, the workers don't talk to me, or even look at me. They stomp past in their rubber suits without even a head nod. They have eyes only for the pigs, and I'm sure they don't trust the boss's wife. They leave me to it.

"New Wife, will you scratch behind my ear?" whines the

mother pig with the high voice, but I can't reach it. There's no room. The mothers lie in tight crates. Without space to move, they must let their urine and feces squirt from their bodies through the grated floor to the concrete below, smearing trails down their skin that irritate and sting. They can't raise their legs to scratch. I imagine the hooves jabbing their uterine walls. I remember pregnancy. I hated every minute.

"New Wife," say the mothers, "where are you from?"

"I am from Hungary," I tell them, extending my hands to stroke the spaces between their eyes. A worker pushes past me, looking down.

"What is Hungary?" they ask.

I speak of my father's map of *Magyar Királyság*, the Kingdom of Hungary – the "real" Hungary, he used to grumble, "to its full extent, before the Treaty carved it up into the little plot of land it is today." That was what he said, right up until he died. My father was not so different from many Hungarians. Even now, if you go into Budapest and you sit down in a dark bar, and you say to the bartender, "Bartender, tell me what Hungary used to be," this bartender will glare at you and bring out his own map of *Magyar Királyság*, and he will say to you, "One day, when we finally rid ourselves of our government, we will be whole again."

The pigs nod, their cheeks brushing the grated floor, though I realize they don't know what a bartender is, or a map, or land.

"We had pigs in Hungary," I say. "They ran the length of forests and found meals in the snow."

"They ran," says the mother who is quiet. "How lovely."

My husband likes to observe rituals when he comes home at the end of the day. He kicks off his muddy boots at the back door, in the "storm room," where one goes to disrobe when they are dirty. (The front door is only for clean entrances.) While I sweep up the crusts of earth, he takes out his small knife and cuts off a piece of the grand soap bowl I made. He scrubs up and down his forearms and soaks them in the sink under hot water for ten minutes. Then, he likes to sit down at the dinner table and eat, in a circle around his plate, the things I've cooked for him: first the meat, then the potatoes, then the vegetables cooked in pig fat. These three actions in this order, every time.

A month into our marriage, I was eager to practice my English. We'd held real conversations only twice, and I wanted to know him. I cooked for my husband one night a lovely mound of pork belly. My father used to call it *Abált szalonna,* boiled bacon anointed with good Hungarian paprika and garlic. Though in Hungary, we ate it cold, I knew my husband hated cold meat, so I served it to him hot with raw slices of onion.

We began our meal in silence. My son loves *Abált szalonna,* and he noisily chewed the tender fat. My husband poked at the rosy lines suspiciously for several minutes. Then he shifted the plate and started with the onions. I ignored his change in routine and kept my hands folded in my lap, where they sweated. I reviewed all my verb tenses.

"Husband," I said slowly. "How was your day?"

My husband snorted and slurped an onion slice. "It was fine. Damn pigs are eating too much, I'll have to cut back on the corn feed I'm getting from Purina."

I understood all the words in his sentence. Pride colored my cheeks.

"Did your father keep pigs also?" I asked. I yearned to know how my husband learned to farm pigs.

"Yeah," said my husband. "Taught me everything I know."

"My father also," I said, pleased.

"Huh," said my husband. "Didn't know that." He looked down at his plate. He turned it again and speared a piece of pork belly with his fork. He bit off an end. "This is good," said my husband.

"My father's recipe," I beamed. I motioned at my son. "We ate it at his birth."

My husband stopped chewing. He stared at me. I frowned. Had I used the wrong tense? Perhaps "birth" was not right, and I should've used "day of birth" instead?

"His birth," mocked my husband. "Was your [word I couldn't remember] there too?"

"My what?" I asked.

My husband was beginning to get impatient. "Your [word I still couldn't remember]."

I sped through all the English words I'd memorized before this conversation, desperate for a familiar definition. The way he'd said it made me think it was a slang term. My husband lost patience. He slammed down his hand.

"His father," he snarled, pointing at my son. I felt the blood flee from my face. A brief image of my son's father – the dark eyes that crinkled joyfully, the one night I saw his naked flesh – flew in and out of my memory. My husband must have seen the image, too. He picked up his plate and threw it at my head. Had I not ducked, it would have shattered my face the way it shattered against the white, tiled wall. My son looked between us, chewing.

"You're with me," said my husband slowly, the way he does when he wants me to know that I am the most stupid of all wives. "Forget him."

I did.

The mothers are bored today. They get to gossiping quickly.

"I want to bite that worker who cleaned my rump this morning," grumbles the mother with the birthmark. "Who uses that much water pressure? I'm still leaking from my asshole."

"Remember when Slackteat licked the blonde one?" says the mother with the tooth-shaped scar on her shoulder.

"How he blushed," says the mother who laughs at everything.

"You would have liked Slackteat, New Wife," says the mother with the scar.

"Slackteat?" I frown.

"One of the ex-wives," says the mother who is sad.

"What happened to her?" I ask.

The mothers shift and twitch their hooves. "Bad blood," they murmur.

"I liked Snowhair," says the mother with the high voice. "Even if she was only around for a month. She was so beautiful."

"Beauty – fuck! We lasted longer than she did!" barks the mother who laughs at everything. The other mothers catch it like children. Their laughter becomes a dull roar.

"Why was Snowhair here a month only?"

"All of us wives get bad blood," says the Quiet Mother. "On every farm in every state." I lean over her crate, but the mothers hear the white food canisters being filled. They swing their necks wildly until their cheeks can touch the tapering mouths of the feeding canisters.

"My hocks are killing me," says the mother who is sad. She sighs.

"Shut it, Slagskin, and eat," snaps the mother with the birthmark. She parts her lips to reveal her white teeth and slavering tongue. She suckles from the great white teat. Gray slop runs down her rosy chin.

Rain will come soon. I walk the path that trails up the hill, and when I am halfway up I stop to look at the house in front of me. The windows, large and clear, give me a yellow glare that cuts the gray evening into pieces. Past the porch, I can see my husband sitting on his leather couch, his face cast blue by the screen in front of him. My son pads over and climbs beside him. He drinks a box of juice. His face begins to blue. I turn away.

The wheat fields bristle up and out like worn, brown fabric. My feet lead me over loose stone and hard earth, away from the confinement. Five feet from the lagoon, the air is suddenly hard with stink. I pull out a rag from the pocket of my jeans and hold it to my nose. I trip and crumple and cough.

At the lip of the water, the trees curl. Grass rots where it touches the still surface. Long, white tubes protrude on stilts, lines of sludge trickling from their lips. I stare at the water. It is the wrong color. It is not dark, not any kind of blue. It is pink. Resting in the purple muck along the shore is a small, pale crescent. I lean down to examine it properly. It is a tiny piglet, a fetus, no larger than my hand, veined, blue-stomached, its legs not quite formed beyond nibs, its eyes squeezed and its mouth stained red with bad, bad blood.

"Mother Pig," I whisper. The mothers are sleeping the fitful sleep of the imprisoned. I want the mother who is quiet, but I cannot find her face in the dark.

"Mother Pig," I whisper.

"New Wife?" someone squeaks. I tiptoe to the left. There: her distinguished cheek, her wide, sad eye roving. I put my mouth close to her ear.

"I saw the lagoon," I murmur. "There was a dead pig."

The Quiet Mother shivers.

"What is the lagoon?" I ask.

"Our waste and our dead and our afterbirths," she says. "The ex-wives. All of us. Every farm has one."

"Every farm?" I whisper. I cannot make sense of the pink poison. Surely I am misunderstanding her English.

The Quiet Mother moans. "Yes, New Wife. Every farm. If you fall in, they won't find your body."

"Slackteat and Snowhair," I say.

"And you," says the mother. "And me."

A light at the end of the confinement clicks on.

"Run," hisses the mother, and so I do.

Our silence could be navigated by ship, it is so wide. I stand beside the bed, naked and ready to fulfill my nightly requirement. My husband stands opposite me in his white boxer shorts, his penis protruding between the short's slit. He rubs his face, the sound of bristles loud in the room.

"Come to bed," he says finally, hauling his body onto the mattress. He kneels in the center, pats the space in front of him. Come here, his hand is saying. But this night is not a night when I can hold my tongue and close my eyes and wait for it all to be over.

"What is the lagoon?" I ask my husband.

"What is the lagoon," my husband repeats.

"Yes," I reply.

"No," he says. "This is like the soap-soup thing. You don't know what you're asking."

"Yes, I do. What is the lagoon?"

"Disrespectful cunt," he says. He raises his hand and brings it down on my face. I laugh.

"I am Hungarian," I remind him. "It will take more than a slap to break me."

"Let's test that theory," he says. His eyes glint.

There are two types of violence to use against a wife.

The first is the smart of the dominating gesture and with it the clarifying pain of understanding one's place, and if it is not beloved, it is at least a learned action.

The second is the pig kind. The flaying of the body. The

butchery. The consumption. The fury.

My husband uses my pig body and leaves me, my mouth stained red, curled on our bloody bed. He locks the door on the way out.

My son scratches at the door.

"Mama," he says quietly.

When I do not answer he tries the handle. It will not open. I lick a corner of the bed sheet and rub at the dried, crusted blood on my inner thighs.

"Mama please, when will he let you out?"

As long as my son still speaks Hungarian, I can continue to lie here silently.

"Hey," booms my jackass husband's voice. "Want to see the pigs?"

My son is led away.

After three days, the door unlocks. My husband stands in the doorway. He hasn't shaved. His beard makes small curls across his ruddy face. He sneers at the sight of me and stomps to our closet. He throws me a white summer dress. It is raining and cold outside.

"Get dressed," says my husband. "We're going to the lagoon."

My husband wears a white mask, but I am forced to hide

my nose in my elbow as we approach the lagoon. It is even pinker than I remembered. The white pipes slip their goop into the sludge. The sun sits high. The flat sky presses down. Standing in rubber suits with masks on their faces are three workers, one much shorter than the other two.

"Mama," shouts the small one, "look at me!"

In his hand is a leash. My eyes follow it to the pig it is attached to.

"New Wife," says the Quiet Mother. Her belly touches the ground, swollen with unborn pigs. My feet sink into the purple muck.

My husband calls to the two workers, "This is the one?" The two workers nod. I have never heard them speak, and even now they stay silent.

"Do it," my husband says.

My son tugs on the leash. The Quiet Mother begins to scream and cry, digging in her heels.

"Please," I say to my husband. I tug on his arm but he wrenches it away. "Son," I yell in Hungarian, "you must stop!"

My son tugs harder. "This is my job, Mama," he pants. "I am learning to be a pig farmer."

I try to move, but my feet are trapped. I am shin deep in the muck of the dead. I watch the workers and my son push and shove the Quiet Mother until only her head can be seen above the pink. She gives me a wild look, and she disappears.

The trees shudder. My son stands. My husband takes my chin in his hand and yanks.

"Disrespect me again, and you go, too," says my husband. His spittle lands on my cheek.

My son looks at me, uncertain, and waves.

I prop open the pen doors. I guide the mothers to standing. I lead the multitude out into the moonlight. I teach them to walk again and then to run. When they run, they carry me on their backs. It's like flying. It's like coming home. I ride the pigs, wild once more, into the brown fabric of this country. The land is ours. The wind is ours. The babies bounce in my arms. The mountains rise from the flat expanse to take us back into their folds. We sleep in a pile of pink, measured breaths. We raise our young to be strong and wild, clever and true. Berries and sweet swamp onions become our meals, and we sing the song of being whole again. My hands teem once more with the smell of slop.

Here is another ending: I prop open my legs. I guide my husband to where he desires. I lead him to the moment when he is grunting and his eyes are closed. I teach my arm to hack the kitchen knife through his thick skin. When he dies, he bleeds all over me. Relief keeps me breathing hard. I drag his body away, wild again, into the pink lagoon. The farm is mine. The pigs are mine. My son rests tight in my arms. The silent workers fade away like shadows at dusk. We work together, my son and

I, in the pens of pink, measured breaths, killing each mother, when her time comes, quietly and eye-to-eye. The meat we now eat comes from peaceful pigs, and there is no fear on my pig farm. My hands teem once more with the smell of slop.

Here is a third: I prop open the oven. I guide my head inside. I lead my hand to the knob. I teach my lungs to stay flat. When I die, I leave no blood. My husband buries my body, wild again, in the black earth. The farm is my son's. The language is his to choose, the television his to watch, the money his to inherit. My husband stands beside him. In the pens of pink, measured breaths, the pigs are silent to my son. There is no shared language there. He spends his life in a country where no one makes their own soap. His hands are clean of everything.

I, New Wife, stand in silence in the cold and the muck. There are three endings for a story like this. I make my choice.

THE GEOTIC BODY

– Give her Jesse, the men chanted. Go on, beat the Jesse out
of her.

I remember rain. It's hard to understand rain in the prairie.

The whore, pressed against the wood shed, lifted her skirts
high above her head—a shield, or surrender: both seemed possible. She wore a ribbon round her neck. Was it to keep her
head from falling off, like in the fable? My heel slid in the mud.
A man looked down at me.

– You should go home, girl.

His fingers played with a coin.

– I'm not a girl, I said.

The men were taunting her.

– Would you like the Jesse beaten out of you?

After, for years, I believed the whore had been like a nesting doll—that she had two people living inside her, one named
Jesse, the other with her Christian name, and that these men
wanted to beat Jesse into a separated existence for sport or some

kind of divine compulsion. Eventually I learned. Jesse meant Hell. The men meant to give her Hell—to beat her so hard, she coughed up her own afterlife.

The whore rolled her eyes.

– Go on then, gentlemen, if you're so jo-fired.

Her skirts did not quiver.

She's unafraid, I thought.

The sky, slavering, pressed down, folded upon the flat land, until the horizon was lost.

Later, the men were tried—a rare moment of justice, a hanging while the sun went down —but the town fixated upon me. Why had a child—dressed only in breeches, no less—watched such a violent affair, and not gone for help, or even screamed? And why, in the aftermath, once the men slunk away, had this child come to the body and grabbed a fistful of the bloody earth, and eaten it right there?

– Let's hope she don't go mad and make a die of it, said the judge, ruling me an innocent. They called me Graveyard from that day on.

So often I dreamt the same dream: a swarm of locusts thick as a mourning sheet, the sky coal-dark, insects skittering somewhere—I could hear them eating and shitting our wheat. I would sink into the pestilential hum, then fall deeper, deeper through time until I felt my own primordial ooze, became a

quivering, half-formed creature still in the womb, a protuber-
ance my mother refused to sing to while her horses freeze to
death at their hitching posts.

I would wake, aware. The first cry I made in this life was in
desire, and the last shall be a response to that call.

The town where we lived had been built on a riverbank, a
small tear in the prairie. People came in wagons, sodbusters settling in homes made of dirt clods, and died with their feet sticking out of the soil. Bounties meant babies. When times were
lean, horses were shot for their meat. Flour was rare. Clothes
wore out. I'm not saying it was simple. I'm saying there was an
order I could not help but break.

For food, I caught ground mice and voles. I caught prairie grouse. I caught passenger pigeons, I roasted the locusts, I
taught myself the ways of wild hares. I fought grass snakes and
won. I followed rattlesnakes to their den, dark nests that stank
sweet, reeked sour, like the hair rimming one's secret holes: I
smelled the rattlesnakes and sang as I speared them, a riot of
hissing down deep in the earth. I couldn't manage deer, bison,
or wolves, but in the end, when we were hungry, my mother coughing up the mess of her chest, it was my catch of rattlesnakes that saved us. I stripped them, fried them with lard
in the pan, browned them, turned them over, browned them
again.

– What is this, said my mother, revolted, jaundiced, jabbing at the seared white meat, but already I had come to crave the poisonous and subterranean. I filled my mouth with snake flesh, rocking my pelvis against the edge of my chair.

– What is this, my mother would say, looking at me, and for her I had no answer.

One day I looked up, milking the cow. In the distance, against the hills downstream, I could see small movements. The wind bore the smell of campfire from some Native settlement nearby.

– Ma, I called. New sodbusters.

Through the window, I heard my mother curse.

I watched the sodbusters approach as I harvested hard knots of potatoes and scattered the feed for the grouse. When at dusk they finally arrived, I counted four - one woman, three girls - hemlines limp, blouses sullied, bare feet crusted with blood and caked in mud.

– Where're your shoes? I asked.

None of them answered.

– We've come far today, said the woman, voice worn.

I stood and wiped myself on my apron. I held out my hand. She took it.

– My mother has made ash cakes, I said: We're out of coffee.

– Thank you, said the woman. A bead of sweat ran down
her wide cheek.

Inside, my mother and I sat on the ground while the sodbusters ate around the fire on our benches, sucking to soften
the hard, unleavened bread. My mother asked their names and
origin. They were a woman called Jane, and her daughters
Miriam, Ellen Madora, Vilate. They'd all come on foot from a
town a few states over, said Jane.

– But that's a month's-worth of walking! my mother ex-
claimed.

And no shoes to do it in, I thought.

– Didn't know Ohio let in folks like you, said my mother.

– They didn't, said Jane, tearing at the burnt edge of ash
cake.

– Let us hope the lords of Belle's Landing can find it in
their hearts to be hospitable, my mother offered.

– Don't set your heart on it, said Jane: They already made
me pay my $500.

My mother grunted and drank from her tin cup.

Jane inspired a curiosity in me that most other people I
knew could not. I was old enough that I'd heard stories of people like her, and the roof of my mouth itched with questions.

– Were you slaves before?

Jane watched me.

– Yes, she said. Her daughters stayed silent, unmoving.

– What kind of slaves were you? The field ones or the house ones?

Jane shoveled crumbs of ash cake onto her pink tongue.

– The kind that should have been freed, she said.

– But how did you get $500? I said.

A silence I caused.

– What's your name? she asked me.

– Graveyard, I said, trying it out. My mother kicked me. Jane raised an eyebrow.

– The townsfolk call her that, said my mother: But I gave her a good Christian name.

I gave Jane my good Christian name.

– -------, Jane repeated.

Then she looked upon me - not at me, or through me, but upon me, as if she had beheld me for a thousand years before this moment and knew she had at least a thousand years left in which she would have to contend with me, with the likes of me, with the many, many likes of me. Outside the crickets spoke in a language I could not fathom.

– ---------, she said at last: You'll do better to treat me with courtesy.

I felt my stomach drop down the well of my body.

– I was only asking, I said.

Jane sat silent. The crickets hummed. The cow lowed in the

barn. I thought of killdeer eggs, clustered together, disguised as stones on the riverbed to hide from the mouths of snakes who always, always found them anyway. My skin itched, as if trying to shed. I saw myself anew.

– I'm sorry, I said.

Jane nodded.

The ash cakes were finished in silence. Then the family rose, and one by one they walked back out into the thick, warm night.

I found a two-headed snake on the red mud riverbank. She writhed and spat, her rattler raised above the sludge. I could not kill her, though hunger was in my gut, for I could see that she was my twin.

The river turned creek, turned trickle, turned dead; all manner of varmint vanished from the landscape; the wind lashed my face. The sky and the plains shared the same jaundiced yellow. Shod homes were abandoned, gusts ripping away the dirt covering the graves and filling the air with uncloaked stench. Some tried to ship in hay for their horses, but the wheels of the caravans could not move for all the dust. I shrank skeletal, unstable stork sifting through the detritus for a locust or beetle to chew. My mother dried up, reduced to a sheet of thin hide curled on the bed. I would pick up her arm and let it drop to her side again.

– Mother, I would say: Mother, tell me what to do.

The days washed together. I couldn't tell you what day it was, what hour, when I stood on trembling legs after digging through an abandoned dugout for food, preparing to crawl home empty handed again.

I raised my eyes. A tall rock, an entire ovoid mountain, floated before me, unanchored.

I only then realized how hungry my eyes had been for a break in the bleak horizon.

The object hovered, somehow both close enough to touch and too far up for even tiptoes. Was it a rock? That word seemed too simple. Who had taught me the word *geode?* Had it been the trapper who'd passed through last winter? I couldn't remember, but it hardly seemed to matter: the word for this tall body was *geode*, I knew. Its exterior, though sloping, seemed dull and jagged, but, as if sliced by the sword of an archangel, the geode was halved, its center revealed. What a paradise within! A grotto made of crystals so lush they burst and broke against each other. A fountain, water pouring pure and fragrant down to wet the dust at my feet. I fell to my knees. A new lake rose to my waist, entered each of my many pores. I felt my skin gulp the wet, felt pleasure wrack my body. I bent my head, and I drank. My flesh swelled.

When I'd had my fill, I crawled forward, hands outstretched.

– Please, I said.

But though I opened my mouth, the heavenly body danced out of my reach.

– Please! I moaned.

The sun vanished behind its great form.

Then I blinked.

When I opened my eyes, the geode had disappeared. In its place were rain clouds.

The river ran with new blood. On the banks a stone sparkled. I picked it up and suckled, an infant teething its bite. My eyes closed. The stone yielded, and my mouth filled with milk. I knew then that I wanted to be like that stone, from here on out – to yield, to feed.

I slipped and slid through the mud, face tipped up, drinking what the sky gave me, and walked toward the hills, the image of Jane and her daughters first walking towards us branded on my memory. I could see a speck in the distance, a possible sod home. I followed the creek. I was right: It led me right to her door. The roof hadn't been finished yet. There were signs of collapse. I resolved to help her fix it.

I knocked on the wood frame and Jane appeared in the doorway.

– I haven't anything, said Jane.

I opened my fist over Jane's hand. As the pink stone fell onto the folds of her skin, sparkling in the weak light, our fingers brushed.

– What a lovely stone, said Jane.

– Sorry, I said, that I'm like this.

– Most of you are.

– I didn't think of you.

– Most of you don't.

– I will learn why.

– Maybe, said Jane: Maybe not.

My words felt backed up in my throat. The hairs on my neck stood painfully, small knives in my flesh. At my back the rain fell. This was the first honest exchange of my life. I felt raw.

From the corner of the sod house came a small, sweet tune, with a melody that climbed like a ladder. I peered into the dim and saw Ellen Madora, sat at a busted piano, fingers moving over the keys. She must have dragged it here from what was once the whorehouse, now a boarded-up shack settled against great dunes of dust. Ellen Madora played two keys together, and the harmony cut through the gloom.

– I had a vision.

Jane waited. Could I say it? I trembled.

– I'm in love with a stone, I confessed at last.

– Ah, said Jane: Love can do wonders for someone like you.

– I love a stone, sang Ellen Madora, her notes high and clear.

The sky wept, the prairie flooded, the gnats returned and, with them, the birds, the fish, the rabbits, the snakes. The geode had given life back to the land. I sat out in the open, day after day, waiting for its return – but the sky swelled only with thunderclouds. I fell into a time of despondency. My mother found her health restored and, now intent on improving my reputation, mistook my misery for the feminine docility she'd always dreamt I could display. She put me in a mended, ill-fitting dress and sent me on foot to the dance hall, where the other remaining young people flocked together to flirt. My hair done in loops I longed to suck, my back to the corner, I had little interest in the human faces before me. I pressed the pebbles I now kept in my bodice, hoping to be left alone.

– It's not that you're not pretty, said the blacksmith's son as he placed his hand on the small of my back. It's just that you're pretty odd for a girl.

– I'm not a girl, I said, tired. His ears went red.

– What can you mean? he said.

A change of hands, of guard, of post.

– My mother told me I had to dance with you, said the butcher's son. His sleeves, rolled to his forearms, looked starched, pristine.

– Very fine, Mr. Olsen, I recited, and ruined the downbeat

with a lock of my knees. I felt him falter. The butcher's son stopped and, stiff, bowed.

I stepped outside and found Ellen Madora, standing by her lonesome beneath the mesquite tree.

– You don't like dancing much, said Ellen Madora.

Her hair was still neat, no sweat on her brow. I gave her my cup of punch and she drank.

– I don't dance well in this body, I replied.

– I'm never asked, she said.

We walked together circling the dance hall, discussing romance. She had never been kissed, she said, having been raised with religious folk who did not approve of their sons kissing freed girls, and now she found herself stuck in a settlement that was seldom different, all things considered. I confessed I had never been kissed, either – not even by my mother.

– But why not? asked Ellen Madora: You're pretty enough. You have lovely eyes.

– Never felt interested, I said, thinking of my geode.

– I suppose now I'll die an old maid, never kissing anyone but the back of my own hand.

She laughed, a small, tinkling laugh that reminded me of her piano. She made me feel bold. With her, I could pretend to know my shape.

– We could learn how to do kiss together.

Ellen Madora tipped her head, the ribbons on her braids

fluttering in a sudden gust.

– That might be nice.

So I leaned down and kissed her. Slowly, her mouth opened to me. I smelled warmth wafting up from the folds of her body, from the crook of her collarbone. When I touched her waist, she pressed herself against me. I wanted to lick her teeth, big white granite, so I did, and she shuddered in my arms. We pulled apart. A spider's web of spit strung between our lips.

– Is it always like that? she whispered. Her nipples hardened beneath my fingers. A rabbit skittered through the dried weeds, and my heart thumped with it. I shook my head – I had no idea.

– Perhaps… perhaps you're a man, then?

I shook my head again. I didn't know how to say it – that I felt closer to rocks than any human name. The pebbles in my bodice grew heavier. I thought I knew what she wanted of me.

– I only know how to touch stones, I said at last: I only know how to drink water.

Ellen Madora took my hand and placed it upon her neck. I felt her swallow, I felt her blood move.

– How do you touch your stone that you love? she asked: How do you drink water?

I pressed my thumb firm against the underside of her chin and felt the hard of her jaw.

– Show me, she pleaded.

The stars burned above us. The music in the dance hall changed tempo, and the people inside hollered with pleasure. Slowly, I reached into my bodice and took out a pebble. She watched me place it on my tongue. My eyelids fluttered as I felt the familiar grit on my teeth, the jagged edges cutting into the roof of my mouth. The milk I tasted tonight was thin and floral. I lolled my tongue in its wet.

Ellen Madora held out her hand, so I reached into my bodice again and handed her my second pebble. She moved the pebble to her mouth. It found its way to her cheek, and I giggled: how sweet she looked, like a child eating too much cake!

– Do you taste it? I said.

But Ellen Madora's face fell. She let the stone fall from her mouth back into her palm.

– What? I asked, my own stone dropping wetly from my lips.

– The stone yields nothing for me, said Ellen Madora.

– But if you just suck differently, I said.

Ellen Madora shook her head.

– If I could show you on your finger, I said.

– Graveyard, she said to me: It's not meant for me. I am barred from it.

A bit of water seeped up from the ground between us where our feet had just trod. Ellen Madora bent down and placed her palm on its surface.

– You can go back into the dance hall if you'd like, she said.

– I'm sorry, I said, but even I heard the empty ring of all my words.

I bent down with her and we gazed at the puddle below, our reflections wavering with each breath we let out.

A wolf, made of many wolves, becomes a pack of wolves. A locust, made of many locusts, becomes a swarm of locusts. A pebble, made of many pebbles, becomes a mountain.

– Stop that, said Mother.

I paused, tongue dug into the pink mudstone. The river lazy, spit's distance from my nose.

– I like it, I said.

– You'll stop with that girl, as well, said Mother.

– I like her, I said.

Her hand came down. Later, I felt tender in the heart of my forehead. A bruise bloom for my turpitudes. A few weeks after, I went to find Ellen Madora, and tell her more about my rocks – but I found their home emptied, the piano still in the corner and missing a few of its keys. And still beyond, through the endless sea of grass, I felt the rocks below, awaiting my mouth.

I began to feel shame, even as I spent more and more nights with rocks in my mouth. My mother said my eyes were turning black with prairie madness, and that soon I would do something stupid, like try to eat a hill and die choking on dirt. I came to believe her: I needed someone to help me comprehend myself.

When I came into my sixteenth birthday, I went to visit the whorehouse, which had been rebuilt since the droughts. I stepped inside and was greeted with dim, red gaslight. The parlor stank. Blankets covered the windows. Customers drank liquor in tumblers and eyed me, dubious, as the women spun naked around the room. The Madam moved about, carrying a tray. I approached her.

— Which are the ones the girls won't touch? I asked as she twirled a customer's mustache.

The Madam pointed. A rumpled corner of men undulated, snorted, all eyes.

— I would like them for my own purposes.

The Madam frowned.

— I won't pay you, she said.

— No need, I replied.

She squinted, then smiled.

— You're the Graveyard.

— Yes.

— Be my guest, she said, and waved her hand.

I approached the corner.

— Gentlemen, I said, I have a proposal.

A pair of eyes opened and closed.

– What have you got down there? they said.

– A banquet hall, I said: I'd like you to fill it.

Another set of eyes opened wide.

– All of us?

– Yes, I said, and began to unlace my bodice: All of you, at once. I should like to be filled properly.

A tongue flashed in the dim lamp light.

– A virgin? one of them croaked.

I merely laughed. What could they know of bodies, of geodes, of swallowing death?

– If you guide me, I said instead: I shall do my best.

When I was naked, clothing pooled at my feet, I let them look upon me. The rumpled corner shuddered. I heard belts unbuckling. Hands, hard and cracked, began petting my legs. Someone pinched my nipple.

In this way, I learned of sex with men.

This, too, though pleasurable, did not cure me. And now all I could see when I closed my eyes was my geode, taunting me, ever out of reach.

How many rocks have I swallowed in my lifetime? What alchemy did I perform, that filled me with such lust? I said this to the apples in the orchard and four fell, rotting. I stood naked in the sun, keening, trying to learn to be worthy of petrification. To the west a dead city, to the east a sick bowl of dust. I dug for the horizon, I plunged my hands into the red mud of my birth and prayed to be made different upon waking. I woke in the dark and walked for miles. I could not understand the limits of what I wanted.

– Graveyard.

I looked up from where I scrubbed the laundry, snow melting on the banks.

– Graveyard, said the oldest of Mitchum's boys: Eat any dead girls lately?

– Just the milliner's pig, I said and scoured my mother's blouse.

– Graveyard, said the oldest boy: Think you can eat this?

I looked up, half-hoping he would toss me some candy. His hands twiddled with the front of his trousers, then revealed a small pink finger of flesh that he began tugging: sad, meager worm in danger of splitting in two. I rolled my eyes. Mitchum's boys hollered.

– Graveyard! said the middle-aged boy: Graveyard, think you can eat this!

He, too, fiddled with the front of his trousers.

– Graveyard! squealed the youngest boy, patting his groin, too young to understand the game afoot but nevertheless eager to inherit the tradition of female harrying.

– Ho ho, I said. I slapped the fabric on the rock beside me, and placed the blouse in my basket. Then I stood.

– Why don't you come over here and find out?

Mitchum's boys faltered. I grinned.

– Walk on the water, sons of Mitchum, I called: And let me show you what I can eat.

Their hands went red as the sun fell behind them.

– Whore! yelled the oldest boy.

I thought of the whore, her brave chin.

– Jesse, I said to myself, and carried my basket back up the banks.

They knocked me down in the snow with a blow to the back of my head, when I was just beyond the vegetable garden. Mitchum's boys knelt on my limbs. The oldest boy loomed above me, breath acrid.

His hand opened to reveal a dead baby killdeer, naked, beak askew, neck snapped and crooked, the corpse a small knot in his palm.

– Open up, Graveyard, said Mitchum's oldest boy.

In response, I bit flesh from his thumb, and swallowed it while he screamed.

I know he hit me, but I cannot remember the pain, nor can I conjure feeling anything else: knuckles, the taste of bird, the crunch of small bones as they forced my jaw to close. I felt none of it. I could only think of the whore, of the bloody dirt sliding down my gullet to crystalize my gut. I became rock, un-flinching, as he hit me. When I opened my eyes some hours later, and found the dead bird still stuffed in my mouth, its foot sticking out between my lips, I swallowed the bird down within me, where I hoped it would be safe, where I hoped it would find a fitting afterlife.

My mother coughed. Her lips left a red continent embla-zoned upon the handkerchief. The wind whistled through the dead grass, the wild rabbit carcasses. I could hear the ants dis-mantling their meager flesh.

– I will ride for the doctor.

– Unlikely, said my mother.

My mother's last words to me were barbed. Even now, I cannot help but feel proud of her.

I sat beside the grave of my mother. I sat beside my moth-er's grave. The moon rose, its teeth at my neck. I had yet to cov-er her body. She lay in the dirt, her soft, mousey curls forming a halo around her head. I couldn't look her in the eye, though I'd left them open. There was still a chance she could wake up and milk the cow – wasn't there? I lowered myself over her head and placed two coins upon her eyes. I'd heard from Ellen Madora that coins helped.

All my life we'd lived together, my mother and I, and now

I couldn't make myself mourn. I grabbed a fistful of dirt and tried to swallow it, but my grief for her was far away. I sat on the edge and dangled my toes against her cold shin. Elsewhere, stars shone.

– I beat the Jesse out of you, Mother, I said.

That was the end of my eulogy.

I heard a great crack then, neither gunshot nor lightning but something deeper that made the crickets go quiet. I looked down at myself and found, with shock, that my body had been halved. Viscera unspooled. I looked into the heart of my split and saw a chasm. A winking purple amethyst lined the center of my body. Bile sat sharp at the back of my throat, an acidic joy: for there, at my center, was everything I had ever consumed. On the rungs of my ribcage, the infant killdeer sat frozen in mid-motion, scuffed-up and worse for the wear, locked in longing with beak agape. The finger flesh of Mitchum's oldest son draped itself elegantly over my liver, like a velvet shawl in a parlor room. The semen of the men at the whorehouse dripped from the shard-tips of my broken sternum, mingling with the milk of countless stones and Ellen Madora's spit. I gazed in awe. I could trace my contents to each moment I'd swallowed – there, too, was the water I'd drunk when the geode first appeared, and there was the milk of our cow, small lakes and puddles in my intestinal caverns; there were all the insects, snakes, rabbits, deer I'd eaten by my own hand, their forms together but still devoid of life. The dirt from the death of the whore. I could still smell her sweet perfume, a copper blood stink in the air.

What had I imagined I'd been giving them, all these forms gathered in my graveyard? What had I taken away? Here they had been all along, nesting inside me: I had never been alone once in my life, their entombment within me complete. I wept with understanding.

Reaching with my right arm into myself, I pulled out the baby killdeer and placed it on the edge of my mother's grave. The crystals cut my thumb, but what are cuts between lovers? I watched as its chest rose and fell, as its eyes blinked, as it raised itself up with a small, piercing chirp and fluttered off into the night. One by one, I reached into my split and brought the other flesh within me back into the world. The snakes shook awake, slithered off through the sweetgrass. The insects and rabbits reformed, scampered. I dug a shallow hole beside my mother's and buried the spit of Ellen Madora, the flesh I'd taken from Mitchum's oldest son, the semen the milk the gifts I'd been given. I emptied my cavern, at last, of life.

When the burying was done, the two shards of my body considered each other. They touched each other's edges. Had they ever met before? They flirted, they pinned one another down into the mud. My righthand fingernail, jagged, caught on a flap of loose left-hand skin and I shouted – the pain became pleasure, and my right side did it again. The wide, terrible sky made space for me and my geodic body as we danced hand in hand in hand in hand, floating above the world as if winged, light, free. My flesh flayed out, my blood and my tears and my milk rained down to the ground, and where it fell, wild roses sprung into existence. I shouted and shuddered. Had I ever been so happy? There I slumbered, at rest, at last.

A pebble, made of many pebbles, becomes a mountain. A grave, made of many graves, becomes a graveyard. A wanting, made of many wantings, becomes a transformation. A transformation is a flight from one place to the next.

ME AND
MONA
AT THE
TABLE

Me and Mona at the table. The table is cheap and made of white wood.

"What? No it's not," says Mona. "This table is an expensive table. It's made of concrete."

Is it?

"Are you serious?"

Mona gets up and leaves. The coffee grows cold. The air around me turns blue. My body goes rabbit, falls numb from the gallop.

Me and Mona at the table. The table is expensive and made of concrete. One of the legs is too short: it wobbles when I try to put my weight on it.

"It is *not* too short," says Mona. "I don't know how you could possibly think I would sit you at a wobbly table."

The air moves into periwinkle. I press my skin together.

Me and Mona at the table. The table is expensive and made

of concrete. All the legs are the appropriate length. Any sensations of wobbling are my own invention.

"But this isn't a table at all," says Mona. "It's a beach towel. We're at the beach."

Me and Mona at the beach. A beach towel is between us, there is no table in sight, I have invented it all, I've been wrong from the start. Why do I feel so tired?

"Finally," says Mona. "See what I'm talking about? A table made of wood. Can you imagine me buying a table made of wood? Are you trying to hurt me?"

No, Mona, I would never want to do that. I'm so sorry!

Me and Mona at – where are we again? I think I know but I'm probably wrong.

"We're at the grocery store, dopey," says Mona.

Me and Mona at the grocery store. Mona's hand is in my armpit. She pinches my skin and I yelp because it hurts.

"No it doesn't," says Mona, "you love when I do that."

Mona pinches my skin and I yelp because it feels so, so good.

"You like that, baby?" says Mona.

Yes, Mona, I love it.

"What do you want for dinner?" says Mona.

I look at the row of fish on ice. The fish are gray, their mouths agape. A single eye apiece glares up at the fluorescents. I pivot to return to the eggplant.

"No, I don't want eggplant," says Mona. "I want fish."

I don't want to eat that fish, Mona, fish makes me feel sick.

"Yes, you do want to eat that fish, you love fish," says Mona.

I want to eat that fish because I love fish.

"Great, let's buy this one."

Yes, Mona, let's buy this one.

Mona, where are we?

"We're in the rain," says Mona, "because you didn't think to bring an umbrella."

Why did I think we'd be inside today? The thunder clatters.

"My dress is soaked," says Mona.

I take off my coat and hold it above her head.

"This isn't working," says Mona, "the rain is blowing sideways."

I take off my pants and wrap them around her.

"Now the wet denim is touching me," says Mona, "and I don't like the feeling."

I lay down in the gutter, where the rain is shoving and pushing into the drain. I become an obstacle, in the way of leaves and cigarette butts.

"Stop being dramatic," says Mona.

What can I do to please you, Mona?

"Jesus, don't say shit like that," says Mona.

I push my wet back into my eyes. Mona grabs my chin.

"Cry, you sissy," says Mona, "cry why don't you."

A tear appears.

Mona grins and releases my chin.

"God I'm so turned on right now."

I'm damp, from the rain or from pleasure – it's hard to tell. I feel confused.

"Tell me you're turned on, too."

I'm turned on, Mona. I am.

Where are we now, Mona?

Mona rolls her eyes while she rolls her cigarette. "We're at your parents' house," Mona hisses. "Jesus."

Where has my mind been these last few weeks? I can't remember if it's spring or fall.

Mona pinches my arm. It feels good. "Ring the doorbell!"

I ring the doorbell.

There are my parents, one red sweater apiece, matching slacks pressed along the seams. I lean close but I don't touch them. A circle of pink light, a spotlight, follows the movements of my wrists as I trace their jaws. I wince, waiting for them to exhibit their expected behavior – but my parents do not move. Their eyes look glassy, like the fish that I love to eat.

These aren't my parents, Mona.

"I know that," says Mona. "Are you crazy?"

I blink and we're at the mall. We're in a violently decorated store. One earring, a black knot, presses into Mona's earlobe, which has swollen into an indignant pink. I have been touching the attendant. I lower my hand.

I'm sorry.

The attendant is angry. The attendant unzips his fly.

"Hey." Mona holds my cheek. "What's going on with you?"

Everything looks blurry. I take my palm and smear the light until we're in a mess of pigment. Is this a church? Are those stained glass windows? Are we in a rose garden? An oil painting?

Mona I don't know where I am. Mona tell me where I am.

We spin and spin and I grow a long pair of ears and leap into my dark mess.

"We're in bed, Jesus, do I have to tell you everything? Why don't you just pay attention?"

I'm sorry, Mona!

"I didn't say anything," says Mona, a strange look on her face.

You didn't? But I could have sworn you did.

Mona shakes her head.

Me and Mona in bed? No one has spoken? Mona takes off her tank top and her tits slap against her belly. I love the way her tits slap against her belly.

"Don't talk about my belly," says Mona, and hides herself. She did say that, right?

Mona takes off her tank top and her tits spring out, they touch nothing, her pink nipples hard and apart, I have never seen nipples as untouchable and apart as these nipples before me.

"Yes," moans Mona, her fingers pinching her nipples. "You've been impossible today. I demand that you say you want to suck my nipples."

I have been impossible today and I want to suck Mona's nipples, so I bend my head to her chest and tongue the taught beads. Mona grasps my head, plunging my face into her flesh.

"Suck them," Mona demands.

I can't breathe, Mona.

"You'll breathe when you suck them."

I suck Mona's nipples.

"Harder."

I suck Mona's nipples harder.

"Harder!"

I suck Mona's nipples as hard as I did when I first came out of my mother's womb. I suck Mona's nipples as hard as I did when I first kissed the girl in the schoolyard and sucked on her tongue like a lolly till she screamed. I suck Mona's nipples so hard that a black sludge begins to seep from their slits into my mouth. It tastes bitter.

"That's not sludge, it's my milk, you brat, and it tastes sweet! Say it tastes sweet!"

Mona's black milk is sweeter than candy, Mona's black milk

gives me cavities, Mona's black milk is so abundant and whole-some that it's all I now need, Mona's black milk is all I need to eat and all I need to breathe, I'm breathing so well I'm getting light-headed, I'm breathing so well I'm losing my vision, black spots dance in front of my eyes and my throat closes up with all that black milk and my stomach churns, an ocean frothing in my gut, my hands are going numb, my hands are going numb, a swirl of black paint wraps like rope around my hips and my hands are going so numb so numb.

Mona tears herself away from my mouth and holds me in front of her, panting. Her eyes are wide.

"Shit," says Mona. "Baby I'm so sorry, are you okay, I'm so sorry!"

We are breaking from our form.

I'm okay.

Mona cups my face in her soft hands.

Mona. Mona I'm scared.

"I love you, baby. Come here. I love you come here."

Mona kisses me up and down my face. She licks my dimples like she's licking frosting from a dish. She strokes my hair and runs her fingernails up and down my neck and I feel my body collect together again. The room sharpens.

"You're my baby," she whispers, "I love you my smallest one."

I want to cry, Mona.

"You can cry. Go ahead, it's okay."

I cry and I cry. I cry tears clear and thin, and when there are none left of that variety I cry thicker, I cry cum-thick, mud-thick, I cry blood and make a stigmata of our tenderness. Mona, Mona, tell me how to dress my wounds.

Mona strokes my hair. She cleans the blood from my cheeks. She leans in close. I feel her eyelashes on my earlobe.

"Remember my limits," whispers Mona. "Remember the game."

I can see where we are, now. A bed skirt falls in front of my nose. Now I can only see her feet, shoved into sensible high heels. I have shrunk. When I look up from beneath the bed where I hide, the ends of a rope dangle down from her hand.

"Can you see where you are?"

I can see where I am.

A rustle. Mona kneels down. The great, unblinking eye.

My Mona looks worn out. My Mona looks familiar.

Mona! I've made you masked, haven't I?

"You can't ask this of me," she says. "It isn't fair."

It isn't fair at all. And yet. You know the way of it. You who sit in bed beside your beloved, listening to their snores, feeling them fart against the side of your thigh, and worry that they will leave you. You who look upon them and fit them with a name made from someone else's face. What a terrible, ravenous mouth love can be: to never desire what's here on the table.

Let's resume the game, Mona. Just a little while longer.

"Very well. Tell me what you want."

Next time go further.

"Further?"

Yes, Mona. Further.

Mona's eyes, so large they could hold a house, grow dark. "What if I killed you next time? Would you like that?"

If you killed me, Mona?

"Yes, you baby, if I killed you."

If you killed me, Mona!

"What if I took a rope and hung you and fucked your dead corpse. What if I took a knife and cut you open so I could suck you out of you. What if I smothered you with a pillow while I punched your thighs, and no matter how hard you clawed at me I didn't stop. Would you like that? Be honest. Would you like that?"

From my mouth comes a famished roar.

Mona. Mona. I would love nothing more.

LITTLE SKIN BAG

Little Skin Bag stood on the stoop, trying to shove the ghost back into her mouth. It was a slippery ghost. It squeaked its tail out from her lips, picked a piece of spinach from her teeth, yawned.

"Fuck off," hissed Little Skin Bag.

Inside the apartment she could hear Cubist spinning disco classics. Shadows of arms akimbo splashed onto the covered windowpanes; every so often a strobe light flashed pink. The ghost laughed in her face with late-night tuna breath. "Too late," declared the ghost. If the ghost had knuckles, it would be cracking them one by one. "Go home and smoke from your roof until your lungs get so black you deflate and fall to your small, pitiful death."

"No. This was a butt-dial," said Little Skin Bag. "Metaphorically."

"The world will be grateful if you never enter this lame shindig," sang the ghost.

This was not going to be like last time. She was not going to freak out. She was not going to get deleted from address books, or email chains, or feeds, or whatever. She would not be a pariah. "Stop freaking me out," she said. "Merry Wife will be here. She likes me."

"Merry Wife," spat the ghost.

"I think she'll leave him," said Little Skin Bag.

"Really."

"You didn't see her face last time," said Little Skin Bag.

"You are so cute," said the ghost. "So cute and so ugly. Not even your mother loves your cute ugly mug."

"Shut up," said Little Skin Bag. "They're coming."

The front door wrenched open. Lips and Right Tit. Black liquid spilled from their red plastic cups. They wore leopard-print dresses tight enough that Little Skin Bag could see pubic bones pronouncing themselves between two pairs of healthy, full thighs. Their mouths were laughing.

"Oh thank God," said Lips, her trademark shade smeared all over her teeth. She swatted playfully at Little Skin Bag's arm. "That *suede!* Ugh. What took you so long!"

"Totally," said Little Skin Bag. She held up her six-pack, which had by now dripped a lake onto the concrete step.

"Oh, I love swill!"

Right Tit grabbed her by the collar and yanked her inside.

"Where's Left Tit?" said Little Skin Bag in the foyer. She blinked four times. It felt like one time too many.

"Stop blinking so much," said the ghost into her ear hair.

"You know her," said Right Tit. "She'd rather watch documentaries about fish. Besides," she added, rubbing her right nipple, "there's only room at this party for one twin, you know?"

Lips nodded, nose scrunched. Little Skin Bag tried not to cringe. She really hated when Right Tit got too drunk. "And Merry Wife?" she asked, going for nonchalant.

"Oh sweetheart," laughed Right Tit. "Merry Wife might not even come, something about Gutting Man being over disco."

Lips rolled her eyes. "He'll show up for the Boar, though."

"There's a Boar at this party?" said Little Skin Bag.

"Totally," said Right Tit.

Lips patted her cheek. "Merry Wife knows where you are. Soon we'll bring out the Boar and you can face fuck that."

Little Skin Bag flushed an ugly color; the ghost rubbed itself on her eczema. She scratched at the patch and a few flakes fell loose onto her shoulders. A roar sounded from the kitchen.

"Oh!" cried Lips and Right Tit.

"I'm gonna go find Cubist," said Little Skin Bag.

"Chill." They nodded.

Little Skin Bag passed through the beaded curtain and into the disco room.

Posters of naked Art Deco models and bands with names like Scourge and Pubic had been taped to the walls. The dance floor was packed with bodies. It stank of spit and sweating creases. From the ceiling hung a black light. She could feel it leeching the color from her skin. She had to get into better lighting, or everyone would think she was always this ugly. She moved towards the back corner.

Cubist was DJing next to a window that had been taped up with cardboard. A pair of white headphones clamped onto his square ears. Little Skin Bag liked Cubist. She watched him swivel his body and thought he was doing an okay job of DJing so far. She was happy for him. Another wave of cheers went up for Chaka Khan. She waved and stepped onto the platform beside his setup.

"Hey hey," yelled Cubist over the music. "Looking mighty baggy tonight."

"Always," answered Little Skin Bag, and she bit down on Cubist's shoulder. "Cool track."

Cubist laughed. "Where's your sweetie?"

Little Skin Bag bit harder.

"Don't you worry." Cubist slid some dials down and up again. "Your secret is safe with me."

Little Skin Bag looked up and happened to catch Collarbone and Carpet stuffing hands through each other's hair. She looked at Cubist and raised an eyebrow.

"It's cool," he said, although his mouth made a movement. "We're not together anymore." He transitioned into a Bhangra classic.

"Hey," she said. "There's a Boar at this party."

"I know!" said Cubist.

"Is it fun, to do the whole Boar thing?" said Little Skin Bag.

Cubist winked at her. "Of course it's fun," he said. "It's their job to make it fun."

Little Skin Bag kissed him on the stubbly cheek and hopped down again. The Oriental area rug under her feet was soaked with liquor slime.

"You know Merry Wife might already be here with Gutting Man," said the ghost. "They might be fucking upstairs in Lips's shower."

"Shut up," said Little Skin Bag. A gust of wind blew up her ponytail and puffed her body. There was a fan in the corner. She knew she should've worn a regular t-shirt. Something that didn't flip so easily. She held down her edges and hoped no one had seen.

The ghost slung a leg from her ear ledge. "You are so ugly under there."

Her skin hurt.

"You should stick your finger down your own throat and pull out your intestines so you stop looking so fat," the ghost suggested.

She wished she could spit into the ghost's mouth. She slid her way through the bodies and back through the veil of the beaded curtain.

Lips and Right Tit were still chatting, slapping each other and sloshing their drinks around, and Little Skin Bag didn't think she could handle anymore of that. She ducked through the swinging door to her right.

The kitchen was bright and the appliances were black and the surfaces were all made of marble. Lips had told Little Skin Bag when she was redoing her kitchen that she liked marble countertops more than any other surface because marble made Lips feel sexy and cold. Little Skin Bag ran a fingertip along a surface. It did feel erotic. She imagined chopping carrots with a nice knife, the sound of blade on polished stone echoing throughout the kitchen.

"Hey, can you open a window?"

Little Skin Bag peered over the other side of the kitchen island. The Boar was there, lying on the tiled floor, legs bound together with white rope.

"Sure thing," said Little Skin Bag, and she walked over to the sink, leaned across the faucet, and popped open the small window there. A wind burst through the opening. The Boar closed its eyes.

"Thanks," said the Boar. "I needed that."

Little Skin Bag sank to the ground and hugged herself. If she had knees, she'd be resting her chin on their crests right now.

"Do you need some water or anything?" she asked the Boar.

The Boar shifted. "Can you turn me so that I can look at you? My eyeballs hurt."

"Sure thing," said Little Skin Bag. She grabbed the Boar by the ankle and gave it a spin. The tusk touching the floor scraped in an unpleasant way, but now she could see the snout and the eyes.

"Thanks," said the Boar.

"No worries," said Little Skin Bag.

They sat for a moment.

"I haven't seen you around," said the Boar.

"Yeah," said Little Skin Bag, "this isn't normally my thing, but I'm supposed to be meeting someone here tonight."

"So you've never seen a Boar before?" said the Boar.

"No," replied Little Skin Bag. "I mean I've heard about it from other people, but I've never seen it in person."

"Well," grunted the Boar. "You'll have to let me know what you think. It isn't for everyone."

"Why not?" said Little Skin Bag.

"You'll see," said the Boar.

"Well, have you been doing this long?" said Little Skin Bag.

"A good while, anyway," said the Boar, rubbing its cheek on the tile. Little Skin Bag reached over and gave its chin a scratch. "Thanks. Yeah, I don't know, it pays the bills and whatever. I mean it sucks, but everything kind of sucks, so I might as well be making a shit ton of money on the party circuits."

"You don't make it sound that fun," said Little Skin Bag, growing uneasy. She could feel that the ghost wanted to make a remark, but she slapped her hair and it stayed quiet.

"That's because it isn't," said the Boar. "Not for me, anyway."

Little Skin Bag fingered her fringe. "What do you do when you aren't working the party circuits?"

The Boar moved its shoulders, which Little Skin Bag interpreted as a shrug. "I like to scream sometimes," it said. "Nothing great. I genuinely believe my screaming isn't worth any fanfare, but it feels good to fill your lungs up like that."

"Where do you like screaming the most?"

"There's a great quarry behind Ray's Auto," said the Boar. "Lots of pink boulders, a little stream when the wet season's in full swing. You can really hear yourself scream down there."

"Wow," said Little Skin Bag.

"Yeah," said the Boar. "What do you do when you're not doing whatever it is that you do?"

Little Skin Bag smoothed her suede and touched her lips to make sure her lip stain hadn't rubbed off. "Well I'm an office assistant at Hval's, but mostly I fuck psychopaths."

The Boar wheezed. "That seems destructive."

Little Skin Bag shifted. "I don't know, it passes the time. It's like you said, everything sucks, so I might as well have a lot of sex."

The Boar looked like it wanted to smile, if it didn't have two curved tusks marring the clean line of its mouth. "Where do you like fucking psychopaths the most?"

Little Skin Bag obliged. "In the dark. Like the real dark, not just a room without the lights on. You know what I mean? Like in geothermal caves on a new moon in the middle of a wolf winter, when light bounces off the snow and no clouds can trap it, and when almost everything is dead. Or in the desert in a canyon that's been dry for a hundred years and not even lizards like to be on those stones anymore."

The Boar raised an eyebrow. "Do you find yourself in conditions like that very often?"

Little Skin Bag shrugged her shoulders. She felt like she might be mirroring the Boar's body language. It felt exciting.

"Have you ever thought about not fucking psychopaths?" the Boar continued. "It seems challenging."

Little Skin Bag stuck her tongue in her cheek. "I mean what can you do, you know? Bodies are particular."

The Boar quieted, and Little Skin Bag shifted onto her other ass cheek. Her calves were beginning to fall asleep, but other than that, she liked talking with the Boar. As long as she didn't think about what would happen to it later, she could pretend it was pleasantly neutral. She felt bold.

"Do you want to see something?" said Little Skin Bag.

"Sure," said the Boar. "Just turn me again."

Little Skin Bag grabbed the Boar's tusk and turned it a little more, so that its black, wet eye stared directly up into her own face. She filled her lungs with a long kitchen breath.

"Don't tell anyone," said Little Skin Bag. Then she lifted the hem of her body and placed it over the Boar's head.

At first the Boar was silent. Little Skin Bag knew what it was going through. The Boar was bearing witness to the great, bleeding eye of her black abyss.

"Holy shit," Little Skin Bag heard from within her bodily space.

She lifted her hem and freed the Boar's head, pressing herself into herself once more. The Boar blinked a bunch.

"Why did you show me that?" asked the Boar. The hairs on its chin quivered. "That felt so personal just then. Do people see you often?"

"No," said Little Skin Bag. "We were having a moment or something. It felt right."

"Wow," said the Boar. "We really were."

They sat in silence.

"It looked so delicate in there," said the Boar.

"Thank you," said Little Skin Bag, touched.

"Don't get used to this," said the ghost, and Little Skin Bag jumped. Luckily, the Boar didn't notice. It was too busy looking down its own snout.

"If you untie me, I'll kiss you for free," said the Boar. "If we're having a moment. You could untie me. We could just put our lips together and be quiet and no one would know, and then

I could leave. They pay me first, you know. I already have the money. It wouldn't be hard to catch a bus at this hour. The 89 still runs."

Little Skin Bag bit her thumb skin. "Come on," she said.

"Sure," said the Boar. "Sorry."

"No, I'm sorry," said Little Skin Bag.

"Listen," said the Boar, "would you mind leaving me alone? I have to mentally prepare myself for this job. I have to do a lot of mental calisthenics. I have to hide in my own unlit caves, you know? And I think it's happening soon. You understand."

Little Skin Bag nodded. She rose to her feet and tiptoed around the island. She slid open the glass door and slipped out into the backyard. Then she pressed it closed again.

"Hey."

Little Skin Bag froze.

"Fuck," said the ghost.

"It's Merry Wife," said Little Skin Bag to the ghost.

"Yeah," said the ghost.

"What do I do?" said Little Skin Bag.

"Kill yourself and hope that's enough," said the ghost.

Little Skin Bag turned around.

Merry Wife. Standing beside a night-blooming cereus. The bowl of the bloom of the nocturnal gooseneck cacti catching the light cast from the kitchens. Mouth so slick. Eyes so green. Nose so long. She wore a translucent black blouse tonight that showed every raised bump on her brown nipples. Her aureoles seemed as big as twin galaxies, and they bounced through the shroud of space beneath her blouse. Merry Wife was now giving her a look that made Little Skin Bag want to suck on her thumb. Her own, or Merry's, or anyone's, really, any thumb would do. Trying for bravado, Little Skin Bag said, "You finally turned up."

Merry Wife cocked her head. "You knew I would," she said, her words prowling into Little Skin Bag's ears, settling on their haunches inside her head, preparing to pounce.

"I don't know what you're going to do," said Little Skin Bag as best as she could.

"No," agreed Merry Wife. "You only hope. You little hopeful bag of skin." She stepped three steps closer.

"Run," said the ghost.

Little Skin Bag felt her back press against the glass. "Come on," she said. "Someone's going to see, and you don't want that, remember?"

"Don't act coy," said Merry Wife. Her feet screamed through the grass.

Little Skin Bag frowned. "You're not listening to me," she said. "I said no more until you break up with Gutting Man."

Merry Wife rolled her eyes. "What he doesn't know," she said. Little Skin Bag only now saw the set of brass rings that Merry Wife wore on her fingers. Little Skin Bag regretted ever leaving the kitchen.

"He said he would gut me," said Little Skin Bag. "Don't you care?"

Merry Wife was close enough to bite her now. She blew a piece of hair off Little Skin Bag's nose. "Not really," she said, in the voice she used when she was also saying eight other things.

Little Skin Bag closed her eyes. She tried to remember how she'd felt only minutes ago.

"The Boar is ready!"

A cheer erupted from the house. Cubist could be heard screeching the records to a halt. Little Skin Bag took the opportunity to open the glass door once more and throw herself back into the kitchen. It now stank of wet yeast and singed fur and hair spray. The crowd had gathered in a circle around the island. She could hear grunts, squeals, loud smacks. She made her way to the front of the crowd. She took a deep breath and tried to hold the air in for as long as possible. She looked up.

On the island, Lips and Right Tit were having a go at the Boar. Right Tit screamed with delight as she rode its wiry-haired back, her bare legs gleaming in the bright kitchen light. Lips knelt in front of the Boar's snout and frenched it with her tongue. Her dress hugged her ass so tight everyone could see the lines of her thong, and most of the eyes were upon this shape. The crowd roared. Money began changing palms. Even Cubist was applauding while Collarbone and Carpet both stroked his square head. Little Skin Bag felt like the only one who could see the Boar's eyes leaked a strange black sludge. Its tusks had been sawed off too close to the bone; the small nubs bled. Lips had done a terrible job at the de-tusking. Little Skin Bag looked away, trying not to feel so nauseous, but Merry Wife stood across from her, staring back. Little Skin Bag swallowed a lump down her throat. That gaze felt like fish hooks digging into her eyelids.

Now Gutting Man emerged from the throng, robed in his usual red. The spurs on his boots made audible clinks. Without taking his eyes off the Boar, he placed one hand on the back of Merry Wife's neck. The other hand lifted the edge of his shirt and scratched at what appeared to be a fresh wound. He tore off the coat of scab; a small tear of blood trickled into the lip of his jeans.

"Fuck," hissed the ghost in her ear. "He knows."

"He does not *know*," said Little Skin Bag. "He doesn't know anything. He's an asshole. Look at those spurs, for fuck's sake. He's a rock. That rock doesn't know shit."

Lips wobbled to her feet again, as if pedestaled, to the raucous applause of the mob.

"Seven whole minutes!" they cried.

"A new record!"

"Three extra points for Right Tit riding its back!"

The Boar lowered its snout, hooves clacking on the marble. Marble no longer seemed erotic to Little Skin Bag.

Lips wiped her wobbly mouth. She held a hand out to Right

Tit and they both clambered down from the island.

"Your turn!" she cried, and pointed right at Little Skin Bag. "French the Boar! French the Boar!"

"French the Boar!" everyone else began to chant.

"I hate parties," said the ghost.

"I'm going to die," said Little Skin Bag.

She looked at the Boar. The Boar looked at her. The Boar seemed miserable. Or maybe Little Skin Bag was only projecting.

She put a hand on the back of its neck. She brought the Boar to the edge of the island.

"I'm sorry," she said to the Boar.

"Not sorry enough to stop," said the Boar, front teeth so pink it broke Little Skin Bag's heart.

"You're right," she said, and placed mouth on snout.

The Boar tasted primarily like that night in The Purest Club when Little Skin Bag and Merry Wife had split a dose of molly and finger-fucked each other in front of the leopard skin nailed to the red, flaking wall. They'd kissed sloppily, heavily, enough to pretend they were devouring one another and skewering one another like kebabs, and this was what the Boar tasted like. The Boar tasted like that feeling. The Boar tasted like the desire for a true dark meat. Little Skin Bag held her mouth as still as possible and kept her eyes shut. *I'm sorry,* she tried to think at the Boar.

"French the Boar, Skin Bag!" she heard Right Tit shouting. "Or it doesn't count!"

"Jesus," said the ghost. "Still glad you came?"

The Boar's front teeth were clenched together and it was impossible to pry them open, no matter how Little Skin Bag cajoled with her tongue, so she settled for making it look like they were tonguing. She rubbed her tongue along the bristled lips, trying not to gag on a stray piece of the Boar's hair. How many minutes had it been? How long could they both hang on? She forgot what she was doing and opened her eyes. The Boar was weeping its black sludge. The wounded nubs where its tusks once curved had reopened and were beginning to bleed.

"Let me help," Little Skin Bag heard Merry Wife say from somewhere beyond this circle of shame. Little Skin Bag felt breasts press into her back, her hair parting at her ear shell.

"Let's have some fun," said Merry Wife.

Little Skin Bag watched Merry Wife's hand reach towards the Boar's ass.

"No!" said Little Skin Bag, but her mouth was full of Boar, and it came out as a gurgle. Merry Wife rubbed herself against Little Skin Bag's back.

"Take it," said Merry Wife. "Both of you."

Little Skin Bag watched in horror as Merry Wife plunged a finger into the Boar's asshole. Then Little Skin Bag swallowed the Boar's screams of pain. She felt sick. She closed her eyes again. She couldn't keep them closed. She opened them. She closed them. She opened them.

"That's right," said Merry Wife. "Remember what I can do to you."

Little Skin Bag tapped the Boar beneath its chin. The Boar looked up, weeping, screaming, tuskless.

"On the count of three," said Little Skin Bag into its teeth, "hide in me like before."

The Boar's eyes were too wide to widen more.

"Wait," said the ghost in her ear.

"One," said Little Skin Bag.

"More!" yelled Lips.

"What are you doing?" said the ghost.

"Two," said Little Skin Bag.

"Do more!" yelled Right Tits.

"Don't you dare," said the ghost.

"Three," said Little Skin Bag.

"You like this," said Merry Wife.

"Now," said Little Skin Bag.

"Fuck," said the ghost.

Little Skin Bag lifted her hem and swallowed the Boar. The island emptied. The crowd roared.

"This isn't going to go well," said the ghost from her earlobe.

"Where is the Boar?" screamed Lips. The neck of her dress had been shoved down below her chest and her nipple glared at Little Skin Bag like a wide, brown eye, a kiss bruise blooming on the base of her throat. Little Skin Bag gulped. She felt the material of her abyss shifting.

"Oh God, I'm getting that Boar out of here," said the ghost.

Don't you dare, she thought. *I can do this.*

"Hey," called the Boar from inside her. "My foot's stuck in your artery."

Little Skin Bag bit down on her tongue. She had to hold herself together.

Merry Wife wrapped her hands around her jaw and yanked her head back. "Are you fucking stupid?" Merry Wife hissed. "Bring the Boar back so we can finish."

Little Skin Bag bit herself harder. Her spit tasted metallic now.

"Hey, something's happening," said the Boar inside her. Her bag body vibrated. *Fuck,* she thought.

"Jesus fucking Christ, why didn't you just rip your intestines out when you had the chance," said the ghost, now deep inside her ear canal. "You are going to fail." Little Skin Bag shuddered. She felt achy.

Merry Wife was clawing at her bag of skin. "Bring it back!" she said, desperation creeping into her voice.

"My hoofs!"

Little Skin Bag closed her eyes, blood spilling into the trough of her mouth. She could picture the Boar staring cross-eyed at its feet, the abyss of her consuming the cartilage from her own membranous fibers. Her hands were cramping with the weight of her edges.

"Skin Bag," said the ghost. "Skin Bag, you have to stop, its legs are melting."

Little Skin Bag grimaced, swallowed.

Suddenly she felt a coldness, an absence behind her. She opened her eyes and turned around. Merry Wife had been dragged back into the arms of the angry crowd, and Gutting Man was bearing down on her with a hooked fingernail, his shirt bearing a perfect line of his own blood. Little Skin Bag opened her mouth.

"If you say anything, you'll lose concentration and the Boar will disappear," said the ghost, sliding around in her frontal lobe. "Which are you saving today? The Boar or Merry Wife?"

Little Skin Bag clamped her lips.

"It's sticky in here," said the Boar, "it's sticking to me, I can't move, it's freaking me out, I'm sinking or melting or something."

"Skin Bag, let the Boar out now," said the ghost.

Little Skin Bag wished she could pet the Boar's bristled head and kiss its snout. She held herself together. *Just let me get outside,* she thought. *Let me get outside and set it free.*

"You're not gonna make it, you fucking idiot, let it out! Skin Bag!" The ghost ricocheted down and over her deviated septum.

Gutting Man advanced on her now. He brought his face close to hers. She was swollen with melting Boar. He could see her ballooning. She held down her edges. She held them down.

"What did I tell you," said Gutting Man.

The Boar struggled within her. Her trachea burned with ghost tail.

"Oh shit," said the ghost. "Oh shit. Come on. Shit."

"Gut her!" cried Right Tit.

Gutting Man grinned. He still had Merry Wife under his fingernails.

"Help!" gasped the Boar. She couldn't feel any more of its kicks. Her abyss must be up to its shoulders now.

Hold yourself together.

Gutting Man held up a finger.

"Where am I going!" cried the Boar.

"Skin Bag," said the ghost.

"It's time to gut you," said Gutting Man.

Little Skin Bag bit off the tip of her tongue. It was all she could think to do. She spat herself into his face, and the tip of her tongue slapped the tip of his nose and tumbled onto the marble tiled floor. Gutting Man blinked, his cheek streaked with black. Bits of her abyss pooled in his philtrum.

"Please!" said the Boar.

Little Skin Bag clenched down.

"Oh," said the ghost.

Gutting Man plunged a needled claw into her suede and dragged down. The crowd around him cheered.

"Fuck," said the ghost.

"Bag!" cried Cubist.

The Boar was silent.

Little Skin Bag slumped. Her abyss spilled from her suede and leaked all over the marble in a pool. It crept towards the first pair of shoes, and the owner bent down to gather it in his hands and rub it into his arms. A lung of hers peeked out, sparkling like black diamonds. The Boar was nowhere to be seen. Gutting Man reached out.

"It's gone," she said. "It isn't here anymore." When she burped, phantasmic bile rose to her molars.

Cubist knelt beside her and held her hand. "What are you doing?" he whispered.

"What did you do with it?" Gutting Man snarled.

Little Skin Bag shrugged. Her eyes felt hot and tender and her skin bag burned at the site of the wound.

"We paid good money for that Boar!" said Right Tit.

"Finish her off!" yelled someone Little Skin Bag didn't know.

Little Skin Bag looked down at her new slit. The mess of her was spattered everywhere. She brought her hands through it. Like black sand, like a fine oil, the texture uncontainable. The ghost curled around her heart muscle, silent. The Boar was somewhere in her. It would never get free. She could close her eyes or keep them open and it wouldn't make a lick of difference.

"What is all this shit?" said Gutting Man, disgust giving him pause.

"True dark meat," said Little Skin Bag, as if from a great distance. She wondered if Lips had special cleaning supplies to get abyss out of marble grout. She wondered if Merry Wife still had asshole gunk on her finger. She wondered what Merry Wife looked like gutted. She tried to look around Gutting Man's form. She couldn't see.

"I'm going to finish you now," said Gutting Man. His grin was back, even with her abyss splattered all over his nice button down. "This is a party, after all."

Little Skin Bag looked around her. Cups were raised high, fresh coats of lipstick were painted onto mouths, hair had been teased into disco shapes and thighs in white pants had formed a forest and she could barely recognize anyone through the angry thicket. Everyone was yelling at her; everyone was saying something. This was a party. And inside her abyss, Little Skin Bag felt a Boar stampede. *Where you're running,* she thought to the Boar of her, *you can make light stick to you forever. That's what it means to fuck a psychopath in deep dark: to look for light that will stick, even when the earth refuses to be hospitable. There's light where you're headed. I did a good thing, right? Didn't I?*

Little Skin Bag looked down. She cupped herself and brought it up to her mouth.

"You can scream if you'd like," said Little Skin Bag to the Boar hiding inside herself.

"Go ahead," said Little Skin Bag.

"Make it a good one," said Little Skin Bag.

Gutting Man bore down.

THE MISDEEDS OF THE ROOT

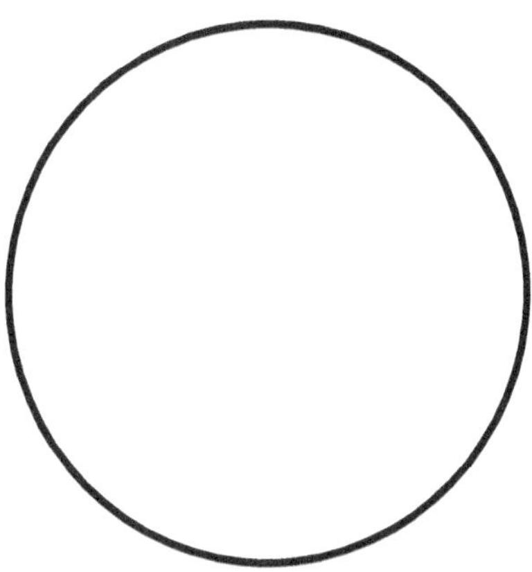

At noon, the women move into the house. It is one story, wooden, abandoned. There are shotgun shells rusting under the deck. Plates have been broken. At the property line: scrub weed overgrowth, a paddock rotting at the joints, earth torn to red and filled with rain in a wide, bloody circle. The air smells sharp, clinging to the memory of horses. The mountains are close. The thunder closer. The women set down their packs.

Look, Jehanne, says the one called Lorraine. A gold-winged warbler.

Jehanne squints.

So it is, says Jehanne.

The gold-winged warbler lifts up from the bee balm and titters a few hundred yards, where it settles on the idea of a truck. The women can see the windshield is broken, but the wheels are intact.

Do you think the engine works? says Lorraine.

I don't know, says Jehanne. She places a hand on Lorraine's shoulder.

The pantry is still filled with tins of food. So is the closet in the hallway: nothing but cans of soup and green beans from floor to ceiling. An ax sits by the wood stove.

Survivalists, suggests Lorraine.

Mice have shat on the kitchen table, eaten holes in the couch, but left the mattress untouched. Lorraine lays down on the mattress and hides herself with the holey quilt. Jehanne touches a coat and moths burst from its chest. In the bathtub, white mushrooms bloom out of the drain.

A quiet sound, repetitive. The honk of a mallard in couplet form.

Can we eat those? asks Jehanne, bending down to peer.

Lorraine strokes her hair.

Jehanne plucks a mushroom.

I think they're oysters, says Lorraine. Perfectly edible. Or they could be poisonous, I can't remember.

As Jehanne stands, the folds of her flatten and release the smell of yeast.

There are no pills left in the cupboards and the mirrors have been broken, but there is a tube of toothpaste in the medicine cabinet, and – prized find – an unused toothbrush. The women straddle the lip of the bathtub and take turns brushing the other's teeth, fingers tilting chins and wiping spare foam, spitting clouds down into the porcelain basin below.

Night comes. The rain grows more fervent. A crack of lightning reveals a mule deer and her fawn eating knotweed. Lorraine finds an old lighter and cooks the bathtub mushrooms in a pan on the stove with the last of the gas. They consume them with their hands. Then they sit on the porch and watch the rain. They lick their lips. Lorraine puts a pot under the gutter. It is soon full.

We'll be happy here, says Lorraine.

I think so, agrees Jehanne, though she eyes the driveway.

A clap of thunder. The trees tremble.

I have to piss, says Jehanne.

Do it here, says Lorraine. I like how it smells.

Jehanne stands up and walks to the edge of the porch, where the floorboards grow soft and rotten. She undoes her jeans and squats. Lorraine crawls forward to close the distance between them. She breathes deep.

Jehanne juts her pelvis and a spray catches Lorraine on the nose. Lorraine laughs.

The women fall asleep on the mattress, their backs pressed. The morning comes crisp. The women, sleepy, try to crawl inside each other's bodies. Lorraine's sinuses are clogged: her head rears above the tangle, snuffling.

Cedar pollen, Jehanne suggests.

Lorraine plugs her left nostril and honks. A crinkle of mucus lands in her hand.

Ugh, says Lorraine.

She wipes the mucus on the side of the mattress, then looks sideways, shy.

Sorry, she says.

In response, Jehanne plugs her own right nostril. Her palms catch a green snarl. On the other side of the mattress, she wipes her own snot.

Now we both live here, says Jehanne.

Their kiss is slow, and a mouse skitters somewhere. In the corner, a beetle rolls a ball of dung.

Lorraine is disturbed by the discovery of the spice rack.

Who leaves behind their spices? she says, lifting glass jars of cinnamon, turmeric, and fennel from the second drawer beside the stove.

Jehanne is preoccupied with the photographs on the mantle. A man in a Stetson stands beside a wagon. There are flowers in the field behind him.

Who, says Lorraine, finding a cast iron skillet in the broiler below the oven, dust caught in its creases: Who leaves behind their skillet?

Jehanne strokes the quilt folded neatly on the back of the lounge chair. The arms are worn down at the ends. Stuffing is escaping the seat.

Like a Rapture, jokes Jehanne.

No cast irons in heaven, laughs Lorraine. She opens a dusty jar with no label and breathes deep. Ground cloves.

Jehanne pushes aside the yellow gingham to watch a falcon hover aloft. The falcon must see a mouse in the meadow. The mountain peak looks a tired kind of blue.

For now we'll just be grateful, says Jehanne to herself.

If I find baking powder I'm making biscuits, says Lorraine.

The falcon dives.

The women walk through the knotweed to the truck, left in the dirt like a seashell. The wheels are frayed and flat. The red paint has chipped and the sides are dinged, the stick shift has rusted into park, the windshield is shattered. Lorraine lifts herself into the passenger seat. Jehanne walks around to the other side, where she pulls herself up by the steering wheel into the driver's position. They sit together. Jehanne plays with the wisps of hair curling at Lorraine's temples.

Remember when we drove to the McDonald Observatory?

You ate that whole bag of Hot Cheetos on the way there. You couldn't stop farting.

And we saw the rings of Saturn, says Lorraine.

Jehanne kisses her forehead.

Lorraine puts her hand on Jehanne's thigh.

I think we're safe, says Lorraine. If you wanted to.

Jehanne takes a deep breath. The wind whistles through the holes in the glass.

Lorraine takes her hand away. Instead, she reaches up and strokes the tendons straining in Jehanne's neck.

The women, barefoot, look down the road. In each direction, the roots of trees have lifted the asphalt by the hems and broken the fabric. An aspen, felled in a storm, hovers precariously just before the westward bend. Dried leaves rattle, bone weary.

We'd hear them first, says Lorraine. She strokes Jehanne's arm.

You're right, says Jehanne.

The women look at one another. Their lips are so close, they could pass one sigh between them. The nettles gasp.

The women stay in the summer mountain house. They begin to indulge in patterns. They grow accustomed to cooking weeds on an open flame in the yard – dandelions, purslane, amaranth, clover. Lorraine finds a bee hive, rank with goldenrod pollen, and the women take to smearing honey on their cheeks. They bleed freely all over the furniture; the mattress grows freckled. They wear the former owners' clothes. The wife's moth-eaten flowered frocks, the husband's undershirts, pants held up by rope knotted at the hip. They sleep soundly, jump on the busted lounge chair, evict the pantry moths, encounter more mushrooms pushing out of the cracking foundation. There are berries bright in the bramble behind the house. The lap of the land provides.

Jehanne unfolds the quilt to shake out the moths and lays it down on the ground outside.

Lorraine, calls Jehanne. She takes off her clothes and folds them neatly.

Lorraine emerges from the house, sun glaring off the dark pubic puff. Amaranth and a pile of bathroom mushrooms that have been cooked on an open flame are now heaped upon the chipped porcelain plate in her arms. Jehanne has filled two cloudy mason jars with fruit wine from the pantry. The women sit naked on the quilt and raise their jars in toast.

Merry Naked Picnic, Jehanne, says Lorraine.

Merry Naked Picnic, Lorraine, says Jehanne.

They clink their jars.

Lorraine comes out from the bedroom, cheeks flushed. Jehanne keeps her attention fixed on the frayed guide to birding in her hands.

I miss our dildos, says Lorraine.

Jehanne turns a page.

It takes forever without them, says Lorraine.

Jehanne bites at the skin in the crease of her thumb.

What if we just did it in the same room, says Lorraine, It would go a lot faster. Maybe I wouldn't be so crabby.

Jehanne puts the guide to birding back on the shelf.

Well? says Lorraine.

We'll see, says Jehanne.

Lorraine smiles and kisses her temple.

On the thirteenth day, in a spell of heat, the women walk to the edge of the paddock, and find a pit. The pit was dug by someone with a shovel. The edges are dulled by the growth of weeds. The skeletons have been picked clean, bleached, and half-buried. Neither cross nor gravestone; the gravedigger had been careless, hurried perhaps. The women bend down and study the bones. Crickets roar, as if signaling a storm, but there are no clouds on the horizon.

Twelve, counts Jehanne. She rubs her neck.

Somewhere, an eagle screams.

Coincidence, says Lorraine. A bad batch.

Pretty bad batch, says Jehanne, and kneels down to push dirt into the hole. Clods of earth rattle into eye sockets.

Husband murders wife, says Lorraine. Sister murders brother.

Maybe, says Jehanne, and pushes more dirt. She thinks of the man in the Stetson on the mantle.

Bad berries. Or cholera. Bacteria. A bear.

Lorraine catches Jehanne's hands.

We're safe here, she says. Can't get sick here.

No, Jehanne says, we aren't safe, not anywhere.

The women scrabble like animals, snagging their finger-nails. It takes them hours of palming the earth and tearing their skin to fill it.

The women sit on the porch and watch the sun die out, slips of spit thick in their mouths. Lorraine plucks a piece of grass and, holding it between her thumbs, presses her lips against the gap. She blows. A sharp scream sound is made.

Don't, says Jehanne.

Lorraine chews on the grass and studies Jehanne's profile.

I feel shocked, says Lorraine.

Jehanne nods. Her scalp feels too tight. She rubs herself. The crickets are in riot: the heat has flattened all possibility of peace. The mushrooms cannot be discouraged. They appear to be bursting from the foundation. Jehanne yanks at the buttons on her shirt and rips it off her body, her chest now bare in the severe dusk. Her nipples peak.

Who dug the grave, says Jehanne, And when?

She cannot stop thinking of the man in the Stetson on the mantle. She can't remember now if all the skulls in the pit were the same size, or different. Had she imagined the identical indent on the brow bone? Had any of them been a different size, or given any indication that these skulls were not all duplicates, multiplicities of one man?

It feels important to know this, says Jehanne.

What can I do? says Lorraine softly.

Jehanne puts her hand on her eyelids. She cries.

Lorraine unbuttons her blouse and lays it down on the porch steps. She crawls to Jehanne. Straddling her lap, she presses their chests together until it hurts. Jehanne buries her face in Lorraine's shoulder.

This is disappointing, weeps Jehanne.

It doesn't mean anything, says Lorraine.

Jehanne pulls back.

Lorraine we saw it, says Jehanne. Lorraine we said. If it ever came to this.

We don't know, insists Lorraine. We aren't scientists.

We don't have to be, says Jehanne. We just have to pay attention.

The women glare at one another, their breasts aching.

We aren't going to agree, says Jehanne finally.

No, agrees Lorraine.

Well then, says Jehanne.

The rest of the evening is spent.

The women go to sleep and when they awaken, they know

things will now feel different. Now it is all negotiation and little to drink. To make matters worse, the rain won't come. Scarcity causes the women to wander, to whine. Jehanne spends afternoons sat at the end of the driveway, watching the road. Lorraine smears her hand with honey and strokes herself, coming in quick, frustrated fits.

They find a lake one afternoon, and though it is too filled with algae to drink, they want to enjoy it nonetheless. They strip down naked and plunge into the water, mud sucking at their heels. Lorraine reaches, but Jehanne dances away.

Move in my direction, says Lorraine.

I am rooted here, says Jehanne.

Jehanne.

Lorraine.

Jehanne cups a breath in the palm of her hand.

Lorraine thrashes. Water is sent into the air.

You don't want me, says Lorraine.

We could be carriers, insists Jehanne.

We came this far! says Lorraine. How far we came, only to be timid in the face of love!

I don't want to kill us, shouts Jehanne.

See the vultures? says Lorraine. See the maggots?

Lorraine climbs out of the water and stomps off into the woods without her clothes.

Jehanne has a nightmare. In the nightmare, the man in the Stetson on the mantle is in bed with the woman from the fridge. Both of them are naked, save the Stetson. The man in the Stetson, atop his wife, plunges himself inside her. She tips her head back. They pant. As they pant, a growth forms on the back of the man in the Stetson's naked thigh, and another man in the Stetson springs forth. The woman from the fridge cries out, and from the center of her forehead comes another woman from the fridge. These new figures grasp for one another and begin to couple. Another man in the Stetson is birthed from a thigh. Another woman from the fridge is birthed from a forehead. Soon the room is overly peopled.

Jehanne, Lorraine is saying: Wake up, you're screaming in my ear.

Each day now, an impossible ask.
I want you.
I want us to live.
Don't you want me?
Don't you trust me?
Please.
No.
The women sleep on separate sides of the mattress.

New rings of mushrooms people the pasture. Orange and

fragile, gray and flat, white cups with pleats ringing the walls of the chalice, long white and narrow tubes, wide red caps, undulating cream waves of more oysters. Strange, that so many mushrooms should grow in spite of this spat of drought: there hasn't been rain for weeks. Lorraine kicks, stomps, uproots.

I am rotting, Lorraine whines. I am a wet log. I am losing my rings.

Jehanne doesn't respond. She rubs at her groin, where her labia are now always coated in a stiff crust of discharge. The house fills with its perfume.

The humidity isn't high, says Jehanne. All these growths.

The fungus are like wolves and your yeast a lone howl, says Lorraine.

Perhaps the moon can cure me, says Jehanne.

Cure, says Lorraine. I hate that word.

One night, unable to sleep, Jehanne can hear a creaking. Might it be cauliflower, edible, creaking as it grows? Or a young and dreamy-eyed doe? She goes to the kitchen, where she finds an old flashlight in a drawer. She turns on the flashlight and comes out to the yard, searing a mushroom cluster with a sharp cone of light. Jehanne sees a cloud surrounding the red cap, undulating outwards. She shifts the light to the other clusters. They, too, are engulfed in the same kind of cloud. The air fills with spore fog.

The women sleep in different rooms.

At midnight, Lorraine tiptoes to the lounge chair. She watches Jehanne's chest rise and fall. The quilt is sliding off her chest. Lorraine gingerly lifts the quilt and tucks Jehanne back in. Jehanne opens her eyes. The women look at one another.

I love you very much, says Lorraine.

I love you very much, says Jehanne.

Lorraine goes back to the bedroom.

Truce? says Jehanne.

Truce, says Lorraine.

They shake on it.

Two gal pals, says Lorraine, smiling.

Two gals bein' pals, finishes Jehanne, smiling.

Their hands warm and between them.

The women have agreed not to fight. They go for another swim. Shy, they change with their backs to one another. The skeeters dart around their intrusions as they step into the lake, shivering. After a moment of quiet, they agree to play a game of light and dark. Lorraine cannot leave the sun, Jehanne must remain in the shadows. They can tease but they cannot touch. The first to leave their territory, loses.

The women jeer, squirt, dance just out of reach. Lorraine

pants, treading water so the muck doesn't touch her feet.

You can look, says Lorraine.

No baiting, says Jehanne. She shivers, and the movement sends the smallest of tides to crash into Lorraine's neck hollow.

Yes, says Lorraine, her hands squeezing her chest. A nipple pops between her thumb and forefinger. Her eyelashes cast shadows. Beat me bloody, my turgid fish.

I can see your cards, says Jehanne, but her hand is absently playing with the curls of her pubic hair, kinked when dry, soft when wet.

The water sloshes.

Can you imagine how wet water moccasins get? Lorraine begins to pant.

Lorraine, says Jehanne, but Lorraine's head has tipped back and her throat is like the moon, pitching light back into the air. Jehanne stumbles and almost leaves the darkness.

Oh yes, all those scales, says Lorraine. She pushes water onto her neck. The black scruff under her armpits gleams in the sun. Oh yes.

Jehanne's fingers are moving in and out of herself. Her opening pulses with a deep, burning itch, and when she thrusts a third finger inside of herself, harsh and unforgiving, she is surprised to find that pain causes her relief. Jehanne keens like a loon. A green, mossy lather gathers between her thighs. She recalls the last time they had sex – a year ago, in their old kitchen, on the floor, a bowl of salad upturned beside them. Jehanne tries to summon a memory of the city. The glass buildings, the bridges, the row houses made of blood red brick. She can see that husband and wife in the park, who screamed at the doubled woman and threw rocks at her until she ran. Jehanne remembers the period of duplicates, seeing a friend at a bakery and then turning the corner and finding the same face repeated. How long they'd hoped it had just been déjà vu. She still smells the acrid stench of their house burning down.

I know we shouldn't, says Lorraine: But don't you want to?

And the memory of Lorraine moaning, the way she shudders when she comes, the mousey smell hiding behind her ears, the sour taste of every crinkle. To crawl inside her again. Jehanne hesitates. A trout comes up for air, snatches a gadfly from the surface of the lake. Lorraine lifts her finger to her own mouth and sucks.

Yes, says Jehanne, and bursts into the sunlight.

Now collide, women's flesh: the breasts the bellies the loins the thighs. Their need is cruel, prophesied, and they bite tug shove to tear and bruise. They push and buck and slide. She forgot the feeling of the other's thighs, hairy, plump, she keened for the crush of a tongue. There is a space between a neck and a shoulder where a lip fits into bone cup. Fingernails – jagged – she cries out at an insular snag, but no stopping. They create a tide. The roots of the trees open to receive it. The sun blots out.

A cloud rises up around them, spray and splatter and mist. A fog settles on the surface of the lake. Thunder. A wind. Here is the moon, waning or waxing, almost invisible beside the peak. A heaving. A moment when the mother multiplies. Thousands of years of volcanic ash and lake silt, disturbed, dance and settle in folds of skin.

Ah.

Ah!

A stillness.

The women cling to one another and pant. The mist around them scatters.

What's? asks Lorraine.

Oh? pants Jehanne.

No yes, Lorraine insists, something…

Oh, says Jehanne, wait, I think I…

The women turn away, backs pressed together. The muscles of their backs ripple, and a retching sound echoes against the trees. From their lips bursts a red mist. It sits above the surface of the water, thick, inert.

Jehanne wraps her arms around Lorraine's waist. Lorraine sighs, pressing herself into Jehanne's lap. Jehanne begins to buck, gentle.

Again, says Lorraine.

Yes, says Jehanne.

Rain falls on the lake and their bodies.

The women do not sleep. The air turns red.

The women awaken to the smell of fungus. Mushrooms have pushed up like ghost bouquets between their legs, against their groins, into the space between their armpits and their elbows, threaded through their hair. These are large, much larger than the bathtub growth, and sturdy. A field mouse finds shelter beneath the white umbrella beside Jehanne's hip. The women laugh and rub against the mushrooms that devour them. Where crushed, a new shoot sprouts up, as if caught in a time lapse. Lorraine, ass in the air, shoves an oyster inside her and plucks it back out again. The suck and release echoes through the forest. Jehanne bends and licks the head. Now they are more frantic, groaning, pressing their bodies into the ground, mushrooms yielding to their plush. A moan – from where does it originate? Clasped hands and grunts, and laughing, and smiling. The aspen grove atwitter. The soil drinking the red, frothy air.

How many days pass of their frolicking, a song upon their lips? How many acres of mushrooms? The grasses thrive, the moss blossoms, the birds all birth, and the hymn of the rhizome is seductive, and even the bees are fooled.

At last, the spore cloud settles and the new growths slow. The women, wordless, naked, rise and make their way towards the house, hand in hand. It is difficult at first to find their footing. The entire forest sits beneath a blanket of white mushrooms. Nothing moves – no wind, no rodent scurry, no bird song. The women are being watched.

They emerge from the woods at dusk to find the old, familiar meadow consumed with fungi. The old truck has all but disappeared beneath the fairy knolls. Lorraine sighs and takes a step forward, but Jehanne grabs her arm.

Love? asks Lorraine.

Look, says Jehanne.

There, on the porch steps of their house, sit two figures.

The figure on the left stands. In their hand is the ax from the kitchen.

It's the owners, says Lorraine.

But Jehanne stays stuck.

It's the neighbors come to check, says Lorraine.

Announce yourselves, yells the figure.

When did this happen, I don't remember this happening, says Jehanne, pulling the hair from the crown of her head.

Who approaches? the figure calls. Their voice sounds familiar.

Oh no, says Lorraine.

A moth sputters through the haze.

Jehanne moves between Lorraine and the house.

Come closer, says the figure.

The figure on the right stands. Their dress ripples, though no wind blows.

Jehanne, says Lorraine. Come away now.

Jehanne looks at her hands, wrinkled and rough from the lack of water.

Yes, says Jehanne.

The women run. Their pace is slow – the mushrooms are thick and thigh-high, and the women must beat the heads with their fists until the rhizomes recoil. The women thrash through the thicket to the lake.

There, on the shore, they see themselves.

Jehanne watches her own mouth bite down on Lorraine's shoulder, her arm around her waist. Lorraine watches her own eyes bulge, her own hips buck. The women hear their own voices come back to them: yes, more, grunts, groans, gasps. Their own naked bodies bucking, the tide lashing their bare flesh.

What is this? whispers Lorraine.

The women watch themselves come, loud and oblivious. For a moment they lay against one another, panting. Then, as before, they watch themselves retch, clouds of red clawing through their throats and spewing into the open.

In the forest, Lorraine clutches her throat.

On the beach, Lorraine looks up.

Behind them, a third Lorraine stands in a dress and gapes.

Six figures stand in the dark red air and recognize.

How many times have the women duplicated, and then flung themselves into exile? Why can they not recall? And which versions are they of themselves? The first? The thirty first? As one version of them runs through the woods, a second version slithers against one another and the third version feels it, quivers in unison, hair rising on their necks, reaching, their memories as blank and untroubled as an open plain.

Root rot. How irrelevant is the origin when faced with the future, incurable and loud?

Three Lorraines and three Jehannes form a geode of gaze.

It's so hard to make sense, whispers Lorraine in the woods, unsure which Lorraine she might be speaking from. Whose mouth is this? Are they all three confused, or is one of them coopting their consciousness?

Jehanne swallows. As if she's grown eyes like a spider, she is aware not just of her own vantage point, but also of those of her duplicates. She lifts a hand and sees in fractals. She wonders if the others in the city had time to be so dazzled by their own conflations, before they shot each other. Or before they died. As is the natural course. Jehanne swallows.

The women in the woods sit down upon a mother log, the other four watching them. The sun will set soon. We bob our heads up and down.

I don't feel uneasy, says Lorraine, her hair caught in the crease of her mouth.

No, agrees Jehanne: Rather, amiable.

I want to please them somehow, says Lorraine. She looks up at the mountainous cleft of Jehanne's chin.

Lorraine leans down and strokes one of our heads, tenderly, and miles away another of us feels her affection and glows. We increase.

Jehanne shivers.

Are you cold, my love? says Lorraine, kissing the sharp neighboring shoulder.

Yes, says Jehanne, I know it's hot but somewhere far off it's cold and I can feel it.

Do you know, says Lorraine, so can I.

We, clever children, lift up our breath, and we mark them with our spores.

Night falls. In the house, the women lay down and kiss tenderly. In the lake, the women press together and kiss tenderly.

In the woods, the women rest and kiss tenderly.

Down below their feet, in each and every location, we har-
vest the seeds we have scattered, and colonize the roots of the
women. We teach them to drink, to fight off diseases. We mutate
their language, we become their language. From each and every
living mouth comes a breath that is ours. Hail mycelia!

We breathe heavy, little lovelorn prepubescent, and in doing
so spit out our spore, small sperm in the spreading dusk. In the
meadow, below the mountain, the women multiply. We watch.
First two, then four, then six, now ten, now twenty. We grow, en-
couraged. We are all of the same root system: we can feel the joy
of the muscles above us. We look up at their naked human flesh.

Jehanne, say ten Lorraines.

Lorraine, say ten Jehannes.

They reach for one another, all twenty, and we toss into the
air our wind, our spores, our seeds for planting. We swell and
engorge. We throb for miles, we can feel it underground, down
where forest fires cannot reach us, down where the worms cannot bite through our veins. We slip our fingers inside our clefts,
we bloom by the lake, we run up the thick thighs of trees, of
mountain peaks. We grow breasts and nipples, we grow pubic
puffs. We press, tight. We scramble up the drain. We sprout up
from the bathtub. We throb. What is felt in the meadow is felt on
the mountain. The wind, our breath, lifts the seed into the air
and tosses them into the wet. Our glossolalia. Pain in the east is

felt in the west. Beyond, the bulbs froth in the dark soil. A bud sits on our chest and screams. We birth it.

PASIPHAE

AN ESSAY

Slavering sea-god sick with rage. My husband at the crux of the sin. And I the one to pay. And I the one to blame. I cannot be made to repent. Did I cast my own curse? The me that emerged, regardless/in spite of, sticky/salted/primed? Fetus me? Fertile me? Are we not mere receptacles for the smear of sacred semen, the whole fabled lot of us fairer sexed? This is my rhetorical thesis. Whether or not I had any say in my actions, whether or not I was cursed by a god, I cannot be made to repent for our love. I will run my mouth to shock them until I rot in death's riverbed.

whore-retrograde

Not to say you weren't a prize. Even my husband, when push came to shove, could not return you to the sea. A real veal vision you made of yourself. Stable dweller. Shackled fighter. Great white accolade. Still dripping from the tip of your tail. Rippled flank. Horns clear as creek water, and no bead of sleep in your lids. Your good eye upon me. Long spools of foreskin. Heft and weight. Estimating, my loose gaze now fixed. The ache of my longing. The ache of it. What I, war bride, was prepared to surrender. A deathless future means no regrets. And my lust, just once, for the upper hand. To literally lust for the feel of the reigns. To get off on the knowledge that this once, it would not be me chomping at the bit. To send my husband spewing poisoned creatures from his proud loins: to do that tenfold, to fuck the gift he was given. Nothing gets me wet like prizewinning.

Let us raise our glasses to the builders. To the father and son. To what I went through to hide my costume of consummation: the prayers I prayed, the price I paid, the nights I spent in my human husband's embrace. He who, without the aid of a skein of liquor, reviled in total this womanly figure. Who busted into me and slept all upon me. No snake or scorpion ejaculate in my cunt, though how poisoned I felt full of kingly juice. To Daedalus and his idiot son and to the plans for a higher contour.

whore-satellite

How I ached. I can't begin to describe it. Repetition gives way to weight. I trembled. I moaned. I mean to tell you I stretched all my holes for you. Don't you wonder how you fit inside me? Hours. Widening myself with candles, root vegetables, handles, trinkets. Sleeping stuffed. The fists of my handmaidens inside me all night, quivering to keep still, fluttering from the effort and disgust they endured. A treasure trove; a cabinet; a preparation; an altar: inside me a carrot, a candle, a rope, a stone, a wild boar's shank bone: polluted to be pure, thusly, for you, how I yearned, for you, Horned One.

whore-math

That equation where you are animal: you are a to b to c: you are fuck to make to earn the meal. The equation where you cannot call me empty, you cannot call me baby, you cannot use me up. And we understood one another, as fellow property that lives and feeds. Desired object of my husband; but in my hands, you switch masters, you turn traitor for me. This is what I loved. This, the threat of your horns.

trojan-whore

Your transformation, my love, will come when your throat is slit and your meat is carved and salted and hung from the spit. But mine was a more majestic trajectory. Picture me provisionally. When the builders bring me to my true form. Immortal bovine shell, never to age, never to die. A regal heifer made from a copse of ash, springing like a babe from the thigh of the earth. The carpenter showed me my new sap-sticky skin: hide so white, fastened, haired roof for my wooden body-house. Soft woods at work here. Whittled haunches, hooves, snout. A lock of false hair. A hole under nose/a hole under tail. To take in breath/ to take in seed. Only two functions required of this new body of mine, and fuck if it didn't feel like a more honest body in the grand scheme of things. I opened the trap door in the belly. Lifted my heel. Clambered inside myself. And once there, smelled the warmed finish. Smooth. With the grain. The hollow center molded to my frame. Arms and legs down heifer trunks. The form I designed. Imagine, my love. To christen a vessel with your own salt. To climb inside, naked and widened, foreign and familiar. To be sealed. Becoming-animal. Beast-makery. Weeping-birth.

I, led by the carpenter to you. You, led by the carpenter to me. We, prepared to earn the meal.

whore-ship

A black-sailed ship will approach on the horizon. A king will drown himself in the sea. A boy will bring out his sword, unravel a spool of thread, slit the neck of a star. Spider Daughter, in charge of a maze, heroine of the story. Starry Son, monster, antagonist. So many sons so slaughtered, so many daughters so left alone to die. I. Irregular Satellite. Misnomer. Bull Adulteress. Can't you see, my love, the origin of my devotion? If I'm to have no other role in this story, then I will fuck until my pubis snaps.

whore-star

Look upon us, I say. Heads tossed/ hooves heaved/ your pheromones thick like a cloud in my nose/ I breathed you in/ one function of this body complete/ the bristle of you audible/ the ache/ unable to wait/ from inside my wooden body I screamed/ you, mounting me/ how you amplified/ how you amplified/ come into me/ you, plunging/ pushing yourself/ through wooden hole to flesh hole/ and here I am ready for you/ so wide/ so ready/ stretched out by vestal virgins and ready for the size of your/ lo/ you slid into me/ slick slack easy/ churned cow butter on a warm wide roll/ cycles of tides, my mouth as a bowl/ so wide was I, the flaps of me fluttered/ a grotto of wet warm worship/ the walls of me yielding/ come into me/ the walls of me quaking/ wild, lo/ spilling with oceans/ the moon all askew/ the tides of us/ the bucking/ the tides of us/ the bucking/ we match/ we make/ the bucking/ the tides of us/ a too-full cup/ lo/ lo/ I say/ the bucking/ bull woman/ bull woman am I:

whore-war

Go on, O Fair, O Just, O Good. Wash your hands of the slop of
me.

Husband, king, voice of my sovereign, "Get out, you whore," an interstellar scream, pounding his man fists on my newfound numb skull. Me inside so sated I am, crying without sound. So filled to the brim I am, leaking. From every place I can, my eyes, my mouth, my loins. My hoof shoes all puddle. My fists full of cream. Laugh of the sea god now loud in my ears. Fetus me! Fertile me! Immortal joke, and I deaf to the punchline! Ha! Ha! Ha!

whore-conclusion

Star offspring. Labyrinthine bedchamber. Meals of children, fed to our child. My milk not for supping. A burst of heat/ blood/ sinew. The builders flee their prison, melt their wings, drown in silence. My king/my husband does well with the whip: "If you want to be a beast, I'll control you like one." Welts and anal bleeding and I long for a variation of your face but if I stick my head into the labyrinth our star child will eat me. He has your snout. He has your hooves. Inclinations and eccentricities. We are all retrograde moons, we have all captured an asteroid. I feel the vacuum of space and time like syphilitic boils on my skin, I have been scrubbed I have been bathed but I am not free of the red root of you, I am a solar god, I turn to myself for light and warmth, I will warm the blistering red point which you extend without thought. And Asterion stalks 7 children in his maze. The star at the center of a subterranean galaxy. Oracular shut-in. Sickle-moon, sky-jaw. Predator, devouring their bread-crumbs in secret behind them. "Which way now," cry the boys; "To the right," tremble the girls; the star child opens his maw. Lo. Lo. History is nothing if not clitoral, and I'll stroke at it till they call me by name. Spit in my mouth. Forget accordingly. I'll bear the fruit. All I'm allowed.

ONE OR SEVERAL DESERTS

The same terms are used to describe ice deserts as sand deserts: there is no line separating earth and sky; there is no intermediate distance, no perspective or contour; visibility is limited; and yet there is an extraordinarily fine topology that relies not on points or objects but rather on haecceities, on sets of relations.

–Gilles Deleuze & Félix Guattari,
A Thousand Plateaus: Capitalism & Schizophrenia

I'm presenting you with my skin. The bare pink flesh of me stripped raw, twitching, oversensitive.

I can look at this cleanly now, with less of the violence that once beset me whenever I called to mind that spring. No longer do I draw hot baths and sit in the water for hours, shivering, the light lazing over the green tiles as I try to recall and recount my transgressions. No longer do I teeter on the very edge of the roof, the city churning below me, smoking a cigarette and wondering how many different pieces of my body I could break before tumbling to my pavement death. No longer do I pull at my flesh and scream. Or rather, not as often.

Though I murder every serpent I see, and, on occasion, I still slaughter horses. You know this, lover. You're the one who washes my shirts.

Night falls, something sets me off, I find a farm and trick a mare with a carrot. And when I smell the blood, and the fresh earth churned up by its desperate kicking, I feel the egg inside of me rising up through my throat. I retch and rejoice, the ovoid heart heavy in the palm of my hand. I drink my fill till the horse is drained, and then I swallow the egg back into my body. I choose this. No one forcing me. I am muscle memory.

Regardless. The time has come. The way of it was this. I will tell you of it, and perhaps, in the telling of it, be rid of it for good.

I'd been traveling out west for an entire year, lugging with me only a single trunkful of books and a satchel of writing utensils, hopping from train to motel to commune to desert to mountain to river to dried lakebed, trying to learn the ways of the neon, crepuscular forms that emerge in such a landscape, and capture them. This was a few years before I'd met you. The land out west is strange. Examples: beasts scaly, horned, hardly furred; the wild sage, thick on the wind; the purple and green cacti which bloom only when unobserved; the drab scrub awash at dusk with violent, dying light.

I wrote some decent lines on the subject, came to enjoy traveling, but ultimately I grew weary of the dry heat and the constant movement. It's as if the desert came to roost in my breast, and slowly but surely I had dried myself out.

It was Anna who greeted me on the train platform to take me in. Perhaps you'd know her under her real name. She was a somewhat famous local actress who contracted a strange and untimely illness, and since then has been rather absent from public memory. I've changed her name here. I am unforgivable in this way and in many others.

A vision in a cool white blouse and a pair of tanned breaches, pale hair loose, her silhouette stark against the poppies that burned upon the hills. Anna, dear Anna, we were once children wrestling in the dirt, our hands grappling at one another, giggling helplessly as the full flesh of her twisted beneath my sweaty palms. Anna, who bunked with me at Horse Camp, who made the smell of hay erotic, who introduced *thirst* and *need*. She filled my head with sound. She rubbed me raw. I cannot tell you my love for you, lover, is the same kind of painful, or that, without her, it would exist at all. I don't know whether this will upset you or not. Generally, I think we don't like being told that a former love was more passionate and damaging than what we can offer, but in this case, I want you to know that I no longer long for a love that will kill me. I have begun to long for life.

But imagine a different version of me, before I knew how to desire kindness. Or safety.

I should clarify. I spent my youth enticing anyone into the river or the bushes or the meadows or the bed. At the time of this story, I was no virgin. I had always harbored few sentimental feelings about the act of intercourse, and since the days of Horse Camp with dear Anna, did not entertain real reverence, but rather ravenous and unrepentant interest. I became practiced.

But then I found, as my youth tapered and my adulthood broadened, that my lust for flesh fell by the wayside. I became a delicate, neutered thing. In the year which contained my travels and my re-acquaintance with Anna, I engaged in consensual acts only twice – once in a saloon, once in a barn with a vagrant – and though I had also been forced to participate in a nonconsensual act of intercourse while out west, I did not dwell on the matter, as I had been told by many that young, slim creatures such as me who choose to travel alone invite violence upon themselves. I came to view the event as my own fault, my own doing, and there can be no space allowed in a person's mind for regret when they receive what they so dutifully asked for. So you read, my darling, a map of my sexual history, and you come to understand that my genitals, at this time, had stopped throbbing ages ago.

But when I saw Anna on the train platform that morning, I felt pressed by the insane desire to fall to her feet and suck her toes until her eyes rolled. I had an image of my tongue, which craved her toe jam, caressing the creases in her skin and softening the dirt beneath her toenails. This sudden onslaught of my rapacious desire – it felt as if I had been blinded, and the sight with which I was restored was absolutely foreign. I could not find myself within my own body. She had snatched my true eyes right out of my head. Now I would have to navigate anew.

Startled and embarrassed, disoriented by these fresh eyes of mine, I trembled, and embraced her with as much sibling affection as I could muster. She laughed and kissed my throat, then held me in front of her.

"You've gotten thin."

Her good eye fixed upon me while her blind eye, pale and unnerving to the inexperienced, stared elsewhere.

"You'll have to fatten me up," I replied. My youthful cleverness makes me cringe to remember it, but Anna threw back that blonde mane and laughed into the dying sun.

We got into her black Buick, and together we began the wind-
ing journey through the woods to the edge of the eastern sea. I
thought fondly of the hours I would spend watching the waves
creep up the black sand and spit out pink, candied kelp. I leaned
forward in my seat, aching to see the red house once more.
Though the western waters had proven themselves powerful under my observation, it was the eastern ones that made me laugh,
quirky thing, full of personality, untamable, true.

"Maxie, I hope you don't mind, but I've got another guest."

"Really?" It wasn't like Anna to invite other guests to stay
during my visits. She knew how deeply I disliked other people,
even then at my most hungry.

"He's painting me." She held the steering wheel with her
elbows in order to better light a cigarette, just narrowly avoid-
ing sending us careening over the cliffs into the terrible crashing
breakers below. "He's staying in the guest room, so I've set up a
little cot for you in the studio. Will that do?"

I said of course that would do, I was so grateful for her hospi-
tality – and to show my gratitude, had purchased several bottles
of a particular kind of alcohol made from the sweet, gooey heart
of the agave plant, which let their green tongues languish upon
the desert floor. An anarchist outside of Laredo had given it to
me as a gift post-coitus.

Anna gasped in delight when I described the woman with a
shaved head and leather, assless chaps. "You darling! You wicked

little creature!" Then she took another drag from her cigarette. "You're going to love him, I think. The painter. He abandoned his law firm to take up painting, he's really got the best mind."

From the corner of my eye, I examined her: tense, excited, girlishly twirling her cigarette between her fingers. "Does he," I said.

"Oh yes, we're quite close. Because of the work, you see, and then afterward we always feel like blowing off steam, so we take a few hours to watch terrible horror films at the theatre just in town. It's exhilarating."

"I didn't know your husband likes horror films."

"Oh no, silly, he doesn't come. He's got work. It's just Lyle and I, eating buckets of popcorn, screaming until we throw up. It's childish. I love it."

She'd done this before. My dear Anna was a bit of a collector. Men and women gathered to her, enraptured by her, caught up in her isolating love, and she consumed them completely before she spat them back out, bedraggled and no longer wanted by anyone. I'd watched this pattern for decades. She was a painter, a dancer, a poet, she could not help her charisma. I had long speculated with our other friends on this aspect of her personality, and how we were just as much a part of her collection as anyone else. And how we loved that, how we felt thrilled by our inclusion. And how we had habits of our own. And how her husband watched, without comment. "Pass the peas, dear." As if everything was under control. Harmless fun.

We pulled into the driveway, the trees thick and roaring in the gusts of wind. Her dog, a cocker spaniel named Eurydice, was overjoyed to see me, and barked excitedly before knocking me down in order to better lick all the months of sweat, grime, and exhaustion from my weathered face. Anna's husband warmly took up my hand in greeting – "Maxie! Always so good to have you" – then lifted my trunk and showed me to the painting studio, which was set off from the main house down a flight of stairs and tucked at the end of a corridor lined with windows. Eurydice and the sound of the sea followed us along our way.

And now, a brief note on homecoming. There is a relief, after so many months of stitching foreign stranger cities and settlements into the fabric of one's life, that blesses a person when they are confronted with absolutely anything familiar. A teacup into which they once plopped sugar can bring them to tears. A pillow into which they once pressed their cheek can now make their chest grow tight. So it was with Anna's studio. The friendly smells of lanolin and walnut oil and turpentine, the rags hanging off shelves and sitting in oily, miserable heaps on the floor, costumes and porcelain props spilling out of large boxes from ballets which she wrote and in which she starred. Unwashed paintbrushes hardened into permanent points of vermillion, winsor lemon, indanthrene. And outside the window, the brilliant sea, a band of color. I felt overcome: with grief, for the conclusion of a wild yet impoverished chapter of my life; with joy, for my return to friends and comfort; with pleasure, for imagining all the writing I could get done at that wooden, paint-spattered desk in the corner with the fine kerosene lamp; with anxiety, that I wouldn't be able to write at all and it would all turn out to be a hobby and I'd have to apply for a secretary position at one of the feeble businesses in town. What complicated joy there is to be found in coming home!

While Eurydice settled herself happily atop my feet, I came to notice some new additions to the studio. A black sheet hung on the wall behind me, and atop a stool rested a very realistic black horse's head, its bald, midnight eye glaring at me. I saw it blink, or I imagined that I did. Which was it? I started.

"Don't mind that, it's for the portrait Lyle is painting." Anna leaned against the doorframe, watching her husband struggle to fit sheets over the camping cot.

"Is it real?" The snout in particular. What dread I felt, looking at that snout. I inched away.

"No, no, it's a mask."

Anna walked over to the horse's head and lifted it with ease. The eye gleamed. She fit it over her head so that the bottom engulfed her neck and rested on her shoulders.

I remember, even now, how desperate I felt for fluidity, for as soon as she donned the mask the air had become a weight, a solid mass. I choked, drowned. The black sheet rippled in an impossible breeze. I stared at Anna's body. Her haunches. Her breasts, straining through the fabric, areolas ever so visible beneath that cool, cool cotton. The barrier between her elegant lines and the hem of the monstrous mask seemed to blur. Half woman, half horse. Suddenly I felt I knew her, this Other Her. The same kind of in-between creature I had always felt myself to be. It felt staggering, overbearingly emotional, to look at someone I'd always known, and to feel that they could finally understand me, at long last, and that I could suddenly understand exactly what it was she wanted. I had a sudden inclination that she wanted to be ridden sidesaddle and have her flesh smacked with a riding crop. I wanted to feel her galloping into my rectum. She wanted to carve out one of my eyes and replace one of the horse's glass eyes with my own. I wanted to shove my entire arm up her cunt and work her like a puppet until she screamed. She wanted to empty her body of its organs and make me sew her beautiful tits to the vacated flesh of her belly. And suddenly the room was gone and there was only the black curtain, wrapped round me like rot. I stared at the horse's head. One of us wanted to behead her. And climb inside her corpse. And live out the rest of our days. Parasitic.

"Please!" I cried.

Eurydice, startled by my vehemence, barked three times. Anna obliged, and the room returned to its previous state of comfort, though now I could feel the atmosphere was tinged with the sour taste of threat.

"I had no idea you hated masks so much," she said, as if she had no inkling of my fright. She cradled the horse head in her arms like a baby before setting it back down on the stool.

I, however, shook like a windowpane in a storm. My heart refused to steady.

"I'm not so fond of it either, dear." Her husband smoothed the quilt on my cot and turned to me, a strange look on his face. "And where are these portraits Lyle has been working on so diligently?" he confided. "It's been five months and I have yet to see any work."

"Five months?" I cried. "And there isn't even a sketch?"

"Excuse me," said Anna, her voice cold. "But I don't believe either of you are painters, so you'll understand if I don't take kindly to your derision."

We both apologized, made amends, and the two of them left me to rest and clean up for supper. Still, I could make myself do neither until I had covered the horse's head with a terrycloth and shoved it behind a stack of emptied paint cans, and had called Eurydice up onto the cot to snuggle against my stomach.

While I napped, I had a nightmare, in which Anna held me and milked me until I bled from my holes. When the first drops of blood turned my milk pink, she finally looked pleased. "From the howling of animals to the wailing of elements and particles," she said, and though I felt it was a familiar line, I knew it was merely prophetic, and would not be written for many years to come. Then she placed a boiled egg inside my mouth and commanded that I swallow. As the egg slid down my gullet, I became empty, vacuous.

When I awoke, it was evening.

We gathered around the dining room table and took our customary seats: Anna's husband at one end, Anna at the other, myself smack-dab in the middle on the left-hand side, and Eurydice fixed at my right, ready for any treat I might – and would – divulge to her. Another place was set with empty cups, a plate, silverware, and a placemat, but the infamous Lyle was nowhere to be found.

Anna nodded sagely. "He won't come until we've started the second course. He hates the salad portion, unless it's drenched in animal fat. In fact," she laughed, "he doesn't much care for anything that isn't drenched in animal fat."

"Indeed," I muttered.

But Lyle missed the first course completely, a beautiful salad composed by Anna's husband of fresh arugula from a farmer down the road mixed with another neighbor's goat cheese, a handful of bright chopped apples, and a splash of lemon olive oil that had been gifted to them by an Italian woman who went to their church. "She's always sending off for expensive olive oils," Anna's husband rolled his eyes, "as if she doesn't have better places to put that money."

"Perhaps this is how she'd like to spend it," Anna replied.

"I don't doubt that it is."

"I don't think you should be judging Mrs. Garza, darling, the act stinks of condescension."

"I wasn't trying to be condescending. Anna. Please."

"Well, that's how I perceived it. Anyway, it isn't our concern how she spends her money. Only that we continue to receive nice olive oil for the table."

I looked down at my plate, embarrassed, and fixated on spearing an apple with the prong of my fork.

"The mushrooms," said Anna's husband, after quietly clearing his throat, "Anna gathered herself from The Chasm, which makes this meal quite haunted, in an interesting sort of way, Maxie."

"The Chasm?" I said.

"Oh yes," said Anna's husband, eyes brightening with enthusiasm. "A gateway to Hell. If you stand atop The Chasm, demons will split your flesh and replicate your soul."

But Anna waved her hand. "Local folklore. It's a rock with a crack in it, no need to be sentimental."

It was during the second course, when Anna was ladling large servings of clam stew – "A local recipe, a much brighter taste than that thick gruel they serve everywhere else" – that a door banged shut and footsteps thudded down the hall. Anna looked up, her chest swelling beneath the fabric of her dress.

"Lyle!" she called in a high voice. "Look who's here!"

Lyle stepped into the dim candlelight.

His features were as follows.

A full, red beard. Eyes green, serpentine. Strong nose. A white, collared shirt rolled up his sizable forearms, the straps of his suspenders slapping his thighs. In the hollow of his throat: a blue circle, tattooed and faded. His lips, deeply embedded in the thicket of his facial jungle, parted to speak.

"Maxie," he said in a soft, Southern voice, and took up my hand. "I've heard so much about you."

I pulled away.

From that point on the three of us were silent, gazing at one another sidelong, as Anna's husband who chattered on about his newfound interest in the oboe. Marine flesh tearing apart between our teeth. It was so strange – as if we had already agreed to what we knew would transpire after our final cocktails, slurped at in the dark, the fire burning a path of light through the windows to the black, churning sea.

We retired to the living room's hearth, hot and bright with roaring flame, for our nightcaps, which Anna's husband fixed for us using an elderberry liqueur he had infused himself with the elderberries growing on the low shrubs in the woods just behind the house. Settled snug into an armchair with Eurydice in my lap, I raised the thick glass to my nose and inhaled the smell of fermented elderberries. When I looked up, I saw Lyle – seated on the edge of his own high-backed armchair, watching me.

"Anna told me you paint," I said to him bluntly. If he thought me simple or fragile, let him be dispelled of that impression straight away. I would hold nothing back for this stranger who had somehow managed to weasel his way into Anna's affections.

Lyle nodded, unblinking.

"Well, what do you paint? If, in fact, you paint anything at all?"

"Goodness, Maxie, how demanding we are!" Anna giggled, already halfway into her second drink. But Lyle kept his face even, sensing I wasn't ready to be playful.

"Still lifes," he murmured.

I raised an eyebrow. "I thought you painted portraits. Aren't you painting Anna's portrait? Or are you as fake a painter as your accent?"

"Maxie!"

Lyle stretched and leaned an elbow on the armrest, and I saw for the first time the seductive qualities of his length, the attraction of that sliver of ankle visible between the hem of his pants and the top of his socks, the delicate, supple beauty of his angular wrists. I felt something stir in the hollow of my throat. I scratched myself savagely. Lyle watched.

"I am not painting a portrait. I am painting a still life."

"How so?"

"Portraits are of people. Still lifes are of objects." Lyle opened his hands.

Eurydice yelped, and I realized I'd been tugging on her ear. I soothed her with my palm. "You're saying," I replied, "Anna is not a person?"

"Not when I'm painting her."

"Excuse me, what the actual hell does that mean?"

"Maxie, please don't be so contemptuous!" Anna, now drunk, stumbled to me, shoved Eurydice to the floor, and curled up in her place on my lap. She bit my collarbone, and I yelped before patting her head a bit awkwardly. Lyle oversaw this exchange, head cocked. I wondered if he ever blinked. I decided to change the subject.

"Where are you from, Lyle?"

Now Lyle looked up at the firelight dancing on the ceiling. "Sand Mountain. Down in Appalachia. Very small, very poor, dirt so red it stains your clothes. The preachers there are snake handlers. You know the term?"

My people being from New England, where a certain collared Protestantism is the way, I shook my head.

"Rattlesnakes, pit vipers, timber rattlers, canebrakes, northern copperheads, cottonmouths," he continued. "These are the snakes they bring into their churches, and in front of their parishioners, in the middle of the service, these preachers handle the snakes, lift them into the air and swing them around without getting bitten or harmed, and in this way they prove that God exists and will bless each and every person in the pews who gives Him their full and undivided faith. It's miracle work. God would never injure a true servant."

"Is that so." I looked closer at his shoes and saw they were simple traveler's boots, though their leather looked stiff-new and their seemed fresh as the day they'd been stitched. "And do you believe in snake handling?"

Lyle laughed, the sound slippery and hard to suss. "There is nothing more honest than snake handling."

"Who'd like another?" Anna's husband crowed from the corner.

"Me, darling, me!" Anna replied in my lap.

"And me," I agreed, holding out my cup.

Halfway through his night cap, Anna's husband suddenly dropped his head to his chest and began snoring deeply. The claret wine trembled in the glasses pressed flush against our skins. We looked at one another.

I awoke the next morning to find my mind wiped blank, and my body naked and bruised. My back was tender, completely untouchable. I stank of sweat and blood and my leg hair, stiff, was plastered to my body with some sort of mucous. My nipples had been ripped ragged: fresh wounds oozed, stung. Something sticky covered my mouth; it would not come off, no matter how hard I rubbed at it with the back of my hand. I tried to stand and immediately felt the urge to retch, as if something sizable was wedged in my throat, but no amount of finger nor fist plunging past the barrier of my tongue could dislodge it. I slapped the side of my head. *Try to remember, Maxie,* I demanded of myself. By chance, I glanced across the room.

The horse head sat in the corner on its perch, smirking. Unbearable. All-knowing.

I pulled on a pair of boots and stumbled out the door, naked, my muscles screaming. The sea was quiet that morning. Fog devoured the coast, I couldn't see beyond the next rocky point on the other side of the small bay. A tangle of red kelp blanketed the beach. The sound of the waves sucking at the debris, sea foam catching and tearing, set my teeth on edge; a strange smell filled the air that reminded me of a horrible, pungent cheese. Even my pubic hair had risen in fright. I could feel myself waiting for something, so I clambered down the shale through wild grass and masses of sea roses, their perfume thick in the air. The wind spat bits of the sea into my face. I don't know how to describe this to you, lover, but I knew what I was looking for. I could feel a body dying somewhere. A large death. It held the wind hostage, the stink, the cheese stink I could only assume was something dead. I climbed over the last shard of shale and found it: white and bloated and stripped of its blue skin. It was a young humpback whale, quite small, almost puppet-like, deposited on its side on the rocks. I sat beside it, breathing in its death gasses, spray flaying my face, for hours.

When I reentered the house, Anna was stationed at the stove, swaddled in a robe and fixing breakfast. I crept through the back door, took a blanket from the sofa, and wrapped it around my naked body. Then I sat huddled at the table and, without speaking, watched her cook. She cracked eggs over the iron skillet, scraped them from the pan, flipped them, moved them to a plate, repeat. It felt entirely familiar, old, warming, as when one plunges one's nose into a quilt which has spent the last 25 years on one's own mother's bed. I felt the tendons of my body begin to relax. But then I watched her pause, suddenly at first and then more frequently, to wince and hold her side.

"Anna?"

She turned to me and winked. "It's nothing. Merely the hazards of womanhood. I must meet with my physician tomorrow."

I asked her next if she'd yet seen the dead whale.

"Oh, those idiot creatures," she said. "I'm so tired of disposing of their carcasses. Can't they die on someone else's beach?"

She lifted two of the plates and carried them to the dining table, motioning for me to join her. We sat, puffed in our swatches of cloth, as she shattered the top of her egg and plunged her small spoon into its heart. Yellow yoke dribbling obscenely down the white, rubbery island.

"Anna."

Mouth full, she lifted her eyes to mine and licked a bit of yoke from the corner of her mouth.

"No need, Maxie. We're all quite fine here." And smiled, slow, before dipping her head to the feast once more.

Do you remember, lover, when you told me of your ex-wife? How she once hit you over the head with a teakettle, locked you in the attic for three days, cheated on you with your brother, kept you from your friends until you woke up one morning and found yourself utterly alone? At first I received all this from you in increments. For six months I waited as you doled out your memories. Then at last, one whiskey evening, you said it all, told me about the time she coerced you, and you could only make it through the telling the once before collapsing for weeks into a debilitating depression, as if drowning in frigid muscle memory, a time during which I gave you sponge baths and fed you nothing but bone broth. When, finally, you gained enough strength to leave your bed, you never spoke of her again. You forbade me to bring up her name. My darling. My beautiful bird. This is the way of it. I can only tell you what we did once. I'm going to wait for just a moment longer. To keep my head above that churning froth.

For seven days and seven nights, we ate dinners of lavish salads and native fish, Eurydice beneath the table, bright eyes watchful for scraps. We drank nightcaps. Sooner and sooner, Anna's husband fell asleep in his chair beside the fire; I wondered so often what Anna used to drug him, what herb she was growing surreptitiously in the garden on the right, southern side of the house. Without speaking, Lyle and Anna took me by the hand. We three retreated to the studio. Night ate its tail. Something occurred. And I woke, with headaches, unable to remember what we'd done, but feeling, nevertheless, hungrier and hungrier with each passing day. And Anna's pain in her side increasing, though she never complained, and in fact she looked happier and happier, as if something was being taken from her which she'd never wanted inside of her in the first place.

Eurydice, too, began acting strange. I would wake up, fall into a pair of wellies, and open the door so that I might tumble to the sea – only to find, sat in my doorway, the tiny toy pup, golden-haired and seething. I would try to lower a hand to pat her head, but she would rear away from me, snarling as she slunk back down the hallway to hide under the couch in the living room. It saddened me to see this change in her. Eurydice and I had always been great friends, kindred spirits, we had shared between us an understanding. In visits prior, she would scramble into my lap and lay her head upon my chest and sigh, deeply, longingly, as if in the cup of my fleshy legs she found respite; and I would mirror her sigh, the bulk of her weight settling the frantic, nervous tic of my heart. And now, for reasons that slid through my memory as sand moves through a sieve, I was losing my connection with this golden-haired creature, this frenetic bird dog, this descendent of the fabled hunters of Eurasian woodcock. It pained me, literally and figuratively, and I bloated and swole with each annex of Eurydice's growls.

Not to mention the animals of all kinds which died on Anna's black, private beach. The humpback whale, rotting away. The seal pups which washed up on the rocks. The dead fawn I found at the edge of the woods, tail tucked under and eye the color of its mother's milk. The bloated fish tangled in seafoam. A distinct lack of birdsong, which made sense when I also came to notice the shattered blue robin's eggs which in the night had been unceremoniously dumped from the scraggly pine at the water's rime onto the kelp-coated shale.

There was an odd moment on the fifth afternoon, when the lot of us were reading by the fire while Anna's husband went into town to purchase ingredients for more extravagant salads, a window cracked so that we could be sung to by the sea. I looked up from my *Collected Willa Cather* to see Anna's fingers stroking the knob of Lyle's knee. I cleared my throat. Both of them looked up, but her hand did not still.

"Anna," I said, raising an eyebrow.

"Yes, Maxie?" She batted her eyelashes, and now her hand crept up his thigh. I could see the mound of him swelling.

I closed my book with a snap and rose from my chair. "No." It was all I could manage, but I hoped my intention was clear: I refused to be triangulated in pretending their apparent affair had any validity. I wasn't certain what part I played in in this, but while I remained conscious, I would not have it.

"No?" Now Anna rose and, before I could stop her, hooked her fingers in the vacant belt loops of my trousers, drawing my hips towards hers. "No? Don't feel left out, Maxie, you're always a part of my heart. Even if I do have a new toy!" She laughed, and I hated her. She ground against me, pelvis pressed into pelvis.

But I was familiar with her games – I'd been playing them since our Camp days, after all – and I tore myself away.

"Anna," I said, not a little breathless, "you must maintain some kind of organization. Please."

I had used a wrong word. Anna's mouth formed a thin, stern, ruddy line.

"*Organization?* And if I am not *organized* enough for you, what do I become? Depraved? Deviant?" Her hands clenched and unclenched. I watched her, uncertain, and before I could stop her, she'd shoved me back down into my chair, the hardbound edges of my book digging into my tailbone.

"If I cannot be nailed down, what do I become, Maxie?" Her cheeks had flushed, the rouge echoing the red velvet of her dressing gown. "If I am not a clear statement, a nice and quiet statement, what am I?" Her breathing grew more labored. "If I give birth to death, what kind of mother can I be?" I couldn't tell whether she felt ill or aroused. I raised a hand to steady her, but she slapped me away. Instead, she leaned down in front of me, hands on the arms of my chair, trapping me, her glorious cleavage hanging low in front of me and, on occasion, brushing the tip of my nose. Anna smiled. "Am I a devil, Maxie? Am I ungodly? Am I, Maxie, Maxie, Maxie?"

My mouth dry, I licked my cracked, peeling lips and clacked my teeth together.

And then she flounced herself down upon my knee, and I felt – with wild, terrified excitement – that she wore no undergarments. I felt the meaty lips of her, the prickly hair of her, the wet, the round thump of her rump, on my bare skin as she ground herself against me: once, twice, thrice, rocking back and forth, golden head thrown back. Panting – I am no longer puzzled by this – "You will be my death, my small, my tiny, my death." Lyle looking on, still as a viper.

The slam of the back door. "Anna, I found spring greens! At this time of year! What a marvel a greenhouse is." Anna's husband rounded the corner and gazed upon the scene. His brow furrowed.

"Anna, dearest," he said, peering down his nose at his wife, "what game are we playing?"

Anna grinned. "Torture the Poet. You love it, don't you, Maxie?"

Her fingernails dug into the skin on my arms.

I cleared my throat. "Yes," I answered. "Invigorating."

"Well," said Anna's husband. "Don't tire yourselves out before dinner, I've quite the treat planned."

"We won't!" Anna sang.

Only when Anna's husband had turned to take his treasures into the kitchen did I shove her off my lap and storm out the door to the beach, Eurydice cowering behind the woodpile no doubt until I'd disappeared from her sight.

And there is one more thing which I wish to say, which may be distasteful to you and polite company, but which bears mentioning: my morning stools, once a familiar brown, became red. A dark, haunting red. And flecked, delicately, with strange, black glops.

On the eighth day, at breakfast, I waited until Anna's husband went out the back door to chop more wood, then I put my fork down on the table. Anna and Lyle both looked up at me, yoke smeared on their chins and cheeks.

"You will stop drugging me," I demanded. "No, don't deny it, Anna, don't you dare. You will stop, at once. You will allow me to remember exactly what it is we're doing every night, or so help me God, I will leave this house and you will never see me again."

Lyle kept perfectly still. I saw in his forearms that his muscles were coiled. I wondered if he would finally strike at me, if he would be so bold while I was still lucid.

"Darling," Anna said, breaking the silence with her tremulous pitch. "It's for your own good."

"So you don't deny it!" I cried. "You've been doing something to me!"

"You've been incredibly willing," she snapped. "Nothing has been *done* to you. You came in *with us* that first night, remember?"

Though most of my mind was up to its familiar tricks – it *was* my fault, I *had* agreed that first day, whether or not I was conscious during the act didn't matter, this was just like out West and I deserved what I got – another voice within me disagreed. *When she drugs you, she gives you no choice. Let her see what you're like without drugs.*

"Show me. Tonight."

Lyle widened his eyes, slowly, until they were the size of two dinner plates. I could see myself in his pupils. "Alright, Maxie. As you wish."

I noted, at the slither of his voice, the stirring in my loins, the dead weight of my stomach. My muscles remembered. A steel trap. While my mind fell apart.

I could barely touch my salad that night, though I tried valiantly – I could not look at Anna's husband without experiencing a flood of pity and sadness for this gentleman. He'd outdone himself this time. Absolute droves of spring greens and tender kale shoots, paired with the last of the season's blueberries, chanterelles chopped and caramelized, robust roasted walnuts, and one of Mrs. Garza's olive oils which, this time, had been infused with lavender. A symphony of seasonal delights. I managed three mouthfuls before I gave up, citing an upset stomach.

A bit of sole, buttered and salted, most of which I placed in Eurydice's bowl while she sat at the other end of the kitchen and shook, and then at long last we were retiring to the hearth for our nightcaps. These, too, I refused, uncertain as I was about Anna's methods and whether or not she'd already spoiled the decanter.

"Poor Maxie," said Anna's husband thickly through his drinker's slur. "We'll have to get you to Anna's physician in the morning."

"Indeed," I said, "if there's anything left of me at all."

Anna's husband, the only one for whom the punchline was

unclear, laughed until his head dropped back and he fell uncon-
scious into a snore.

The fire roared.

"Before we begin," I said. "I'm curious. What is it you drug him with?"

Lyle, grim-faced, folded his arms. "He drugs himself. The coward." Anna touched his elbow.

"What?" I sputtered.

"Valerian root," Anna replied. "He knocks himself out so he doesn't have to hear us."

"He knows?"

"Of course he knows." She pursed her lips. "I asked him. He declined."

I looked down at the slumbering form of her husband. I had misjudged him completely.

"Come," said Lyle. He held out his hand and as I took it his warm heat enveloped my small palm.

Together, we all three entered the studio.

When we closed the door, Eurydice began barking, desperately, repeatedly. A series of cushioned thuds: presumably, as she threw her tiny yellow body against the door. Then a yelp.

"Eurydice, dear!" I turned towards the door, concerned she might have injured herself, but Anna clasped my forearm and I was forced to halt.

"She's just a dog," said Anna distastefully.

Eurydice whimpered, fell silent.

When we entered the studio I searched for signs of what was about to transpire. Nothing seemed out of place: quilts crumpled on my cot, my suitcases of books and trousers overflowing beneath, the mirror, the black backdrop. The stink of paints, oils, turpentine. The horse head. Beady eyed. Smug.

When they moved, it was with a precision, as if choreographed. Anna moved to the stool where sat the horse head while Lyle positioned himself in the center of the room. He knelt down, removed his shoes and his stockings. With a piece of red chalk from his pocket, he drew a full circle around himself, flanked by two crescents. Then, from the other pocket, he withdrew a handful of salt. He rose and, hunched like an old man, trickled a white line through the heart of the formation.

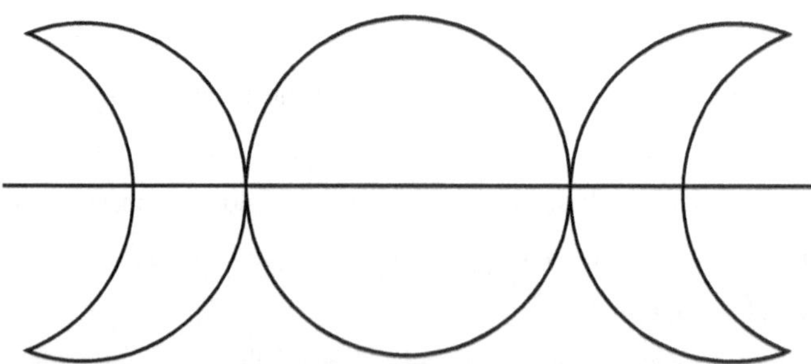

The arrangement of the shapes was familiar to me, trained as I was in the Classics. My mind moved frenetically, leaping between phrases and images I knew: Triple Goddess Moon, Artemis/Selene/Hecate, Maiden/Mother/Crone, *Diana in the leaves so green, Luna that so bright doth sheen, Persephone in Hell...* This was the Feminine Divine. I'd never felt comfortable engaging with this kind of paganism, uncertain as I was about where I fit within its confines. I bit savagely at the flesh beneath my fingernails in an attempt to steady my thoughts with pain.

I hadn't minded the formation, felt comforted by it even – perhaps this was simpler than I'd thought, perhaps all this studio time involved was dressed-up sexual engagement – until Lyle laid down the salt. That white, negating line. This kind of line concerned me: what did a striking of ancient, natural order look like, why would Anna be interested in traversing through the Feminine Divine from birth to motherhood to death each night? Her words echoed in my head: *If I am not organized, what do I become?* I yearned for sleep to wake years later, when all three of them had moved out and I could be left alone in peace. Anna's hand drew/moved down the snout of the horse, slow and sensual. I felt a twinge in my groin. Why, with her, could I never leave well enough alone? Why did she always make me slaver? I detested myself in that moment. As if the stink of the nest of me was suddenly too potent to inhale. I wanted to crawl into the heart of the Earth, where there were only stones and worms, and die an odorless death.

When the floor markings were finished, Lyle positioned himself within the crescent to the left of the full moon. He looked at me and beckoned.

"Death, stand at my opposite."

"'Death?' Why must I be Death?" This was met with silent derision. There was, apparently, no space for laughter in their secret ritual. Rolling my eyes, I moved myself until I assumed the role of Death within the opposite crescent.

I looked to Lyle, who nodded.

"Death, remove your clothing."

"Absolutely not," I said.

"This is required."

With every passing second, I felt more and more like punching him in the face. "I've done this every night for the past week?"

I felt Anna's hand at my back, her lips press against the cockle shell of my ear. "Yes, darling. This is how these things go."

"These *things?* Anna..."

Her hand pressed harder into the ridges of my spine, then traveled down to my waist. The heat of her breath startled me; the hairs on the nape of my neck rose in spite of themselves. "Maxie," she purred. "Show me your body. I love to see your body."

I swallowed.

Though what comes later is mystifying in its derangement, the true horror for me began here, with stripping myself in front of Lyle and Anna. You'll remember when we first coupled, lover: it scares me to be looked at. When you held me still by the hips and said you wanted to look at me, even with the whiskey in my blood I shook like an aspen in a storm. That night, I hadn't a single drop of alcohol in my blood to dull the sharpness of meeting Lyle's dark, probing gaze, our hands peeling away the shells of ourselves – for he, too, was stripping. I had the urge to wrap my arms around myself, to hide the architecture of my flesh. I felt my blood panic, pounding in my ears, but I couldn't look away, each of us set as we were in roles already in motion, the two of them in on the secret and I their vestal virgin, ripe for induction. My mind detached. The ghost of a pair of unwanted hands fluttered around my waist.

We stood in the hearts of two opposing crescents, naked and waiting.

"Mother," said Lyle. "Enter your moon."

Anna, holding the horse head, moved into the full moon. Together, we formed a line, planetary in our alignment.

A wind stirred in the room, disturbed the black cloth behind Anna, though the window was shut tight. Far off in the distance a boat moaned. Anna set down the horse head and reached for the bow at her waist. I could smell her perfume, tangerine and bergamot, thick, full with the heat of her body. A pert breast, a large, brown areola, a nipple sharp and hard. The elegant curve of her collar bone. The slope of her slack belly. The dark, thick, pungent meadow of her loins. She unwrapped the dress from her body, let the flowered fabric crumple behind her. I could barely breathe, I was of two minds.

"Rent the knot."

I looked at Lyle. *Rent the knot?* I tried to shift my posture, but Lyle and Anna opened their palms, and I found my own mirroring the motion, of their own accord. My chest tightened.

"Rent the knot."

Another gust of wind. Eurydice weeping at the door. I tried to regain control of my limbs, heart pounding, but they would not obey me; they longed to follow their leader, muscle memory. I couldn't do this again, lover, you understand, I could not and would not do this again.

"Rent the knot."

Then he turned to Anna, and nodded. Anna lifted the horse's head.

"Wait," I said, or thought, for my mouth would not move, though my voice echoed in the chamber nonetheless, I wanted to beg for reprieve, or something, what was it I wanted to beg for, I did not want this after all, I wanted out, couldn't they see I wanted out, perhaps it wasn't too late to drug myself, I tried my very best to lift my feet and run from – but before I could free myself, Anna slipped the mask down over her face, and so, internally kicking and screaming, I was dragged like Persephone from this plane of existence, down, down, down into that cursèd, nightmare underworld.

A sound, slanted, crooked, kinked:

/////////////////////////
/////////////////////////
/////////////////////////

It came from my mouth. Like tails of garlic trailing down into
the black.

Not so much darkness as a removal of space and time. A winking out. Lack of light. My surroundings wisped away, as if they'd been made of smoke all along. The air, too, changed, turned solid, and all moisture in my body sucked out through my pores, leathered me out. I was a wound in space and the air curled around me, trying to scab the lesion I left. The red lines of the moons glowed, the white line of salt burned bright as a lamp. Anna to my left, lit by the lines, haunches rippling, tossing her head, nipples hard enough to prong my tongue, I wanted to split my tongue on her, to cut myself sucking her limp. The full bush of her between her legs, untrimmed, undefined. I longed to plunge my fingers into their tufts. Tuck my nose into their timberland, root out the truffle. Familiar sensations. I've thought this before. If my hips could move they would buck, for the same wild images passing through my mind, riding her stitching her limb to limb slick slide slop until my fingertips emerge from her eye sockets, until they peer out from her nose, until my entire hand ruptures the velvet lining of her soul and her cries become screams. I am sweating with exertion, with glut. I gasp. I flounder.

"Look down."

Lyle. I bend my neck to his wishes. Is he the master? I feel anger flare in my chest, but when I try to voice it, my tongue becomes elongated, flickers from my lips, and I find it's been split after all. Have I already bit at her nipple, and forgotten?

"///////////////////////?" I say. Pleasure gallops throughout my body. This language suits me.

"Death and Birth will now commence with meeting their Mother," Lyle replies.

The salt leads to Anna. She snorts, whinnies. Paws the ground. I can feel ripples in the air, tides of heat, her cunt opening, closing, night bloom, Datura, vespertine poison, cool shade drink. My feet begin to move.

I did what was asked of me. I walked the salt line.

My language is thin skinned. Is shedding.

Forgive me for this, o, forgive me.

A roar within me, the light, salt light in Hell, Lyle's length resting upon her swollen thigh, & I pressed so tight against her hip her movements send shivers into my sex, ready for the feed for the gift. My teeth keening … Tongue aflicker … If I can move down to bite supple shoulder. It is hard to hold the language line.

"Birth Child will mount its mother and call forth the eggs," says Lyle. This is what is happening now or then …

I mean that I watched …

That I let …

O! Lover!

Lover—

Anna turns her head, ears twitching tosses her mane rocks her rump back & forth in the air nipple knives weep milk for the mouth of her child/to harm the mouth of her child[ren] … Lyle's cock dancing foxtrot up & down head pearling supper for the equine entrance …   He now enters the full moon phase body transforms how can I say it?

body becomes   —   a flower   —   stud bud

—   nightshade   —

          Datura —   lining her body with his   — white —

paint

five-petaled yellow stamen puff of powder release and lift milk —

lifts his mother &   —

meeeeeeeeeeets her upon his stem meeeeeeeeeeets her I watch
him meeeeeeeeeeet her how can his eyes be upon mine and
hers?////he is saying something with his lips —I watch him say
it O—he sayso—up & down his snout////slides her—mother infant
injection drink it, Mother, drink from his chalice—she holds him
within her—her haunches squeeze—
//to let/
// //////////////////////////////////////
//
/////////////////////////////////////me//
// /////////
//
//
//   ////////////////////////////////me mine
hold// //
///
//
//
//slides her—mother//////////////////////
//
//lover I'm/////////////////////
/// /////////////////////////////////
//
//
/////////////////

///
///
///////////// sssssssssssssssssssssssssssssssssssssory //////////////////////////////////////
//
///
// /////////
//
///
///
///
///
///
///
///
//&///
///////////////////////////
///
///
///&/////////////////////////////////
///

now — forgive me — thirst!— mine me my turn my turn gyve me

I keen ancient old child tongue of the crone split in two pronged

a whistle will he , , , gyve , , , me will he , , , gyv v v ve , , , me

permission

It is hard to say this —

It is hard …

//

///////////////////////////////////////

//

//

//

///

"Crone Child will enter its mother and devour the eggs," says Lyle—

—in this dark desert I return, in this dark desert prickled plants scream of night I return to snap the fingers of the ghost hands I asked to invade me—

///

//

I do the —invading //

///

//

///

It is hard! O Lover! I want it —

I want it —

It is by my choice that I do so

…that I do so thusly…

//

///

I Crone Child enter the full, pregnant moon —

anna dripping juice down her legs ass still clenching unclenching
with joy of eros clench unclench red rose bud alert
—   flesh stink of the mother uterus piquant in desert
airpromise of water trust water   —

to sew her ass to her knees —
to eat out her organ[ization]s —
"tramp deviant" —
— "yes" anna mare sound says —

annamama//I am death I bring
  death to o///////////////////////////// my body waning gibbous turn
      now to transform , tongue pronged , tongue split serpentine
      plinth of me obelisk basilisk precious unhinging , , , / hinge of
      the jaw unlock body unlock unlock ////////////////////////// I say
  thus I say ////////////////// bend to the meadow , great meadow of
      the western plains , , anna mare sound here, , , the only way
      I can tell it darling darling dddddddarling , , my turnnnnnnn-
      nnn to invade . ! . slither up her slickened thighs curl around
  sqeeeeeeeeeeeeeeze , , , ! DEATH of of of , , , , , anna mare sound
  here, , , white plump flesh cut off blood looooooosen travel soft
      flesh here small bites ////////////////////////////// anna mare sound
  here , , , canals and crevices wet squick slop child mess /////// , , ,

, , , lips lips fragile curtains BITE , , anna mare sound here , , ,

corpse made easy to slide up into body meeeeeeeeeeeeeet up

into body in out obelisk basilisk slurp the soup of man & woman

can I make it lesssssssssssssssssssssssss —

how can I make it lesssssssssssssssssssssssssssssssssss —

obelisk basilisk //

obelisk basilisk //

undoes the knot

&

roots out the eggs

‡

meat nest

Δ

egg feast

Ø

sulphuric

§

empty meat nest

Ω

eat each glop egg slop egg rot

œ

anna mare sound here

∫

anna mare sound here

∫

obelisk basilisk slither sly slip slop slap slink slowly south stuffed
with mare birth satiated sated slaked of thirst obelisk basilisk
lovingly jaw unhinged snap snip sew the flesh shut needle teeth
thread anna mare sound here tail tail? tail curl slide in and out —

    — "Crone Child will swallow Mother's young"
down length of sssssslim ssssssssswole tube, , , , , no cham-
bersssssssss , , , , to arresssssssst , , , , movement slid up anna mare
body, curled around throat, anna mare sound here anna mare
sound here tail meeeeeeeeeeting her below my pronged tongue
meeeeeeeeeeeeeeeeeeting her above lack of ssssssssssssshape lack
of organization Birth Child behind her here issssssssss ssssssssss-
something more recognizsssssssssable more recognizssssssssssssable
three of ussssssssss three of usssssssssssss hold on to that alright yes
ssssssssssssssssssssssssssssssssssssssssssss

    —

O!

mother: hold me by head: "make me

without"   "make me a ewer"   "make of me passage"

"maxie"   "empty me out"   "flay me"

        "venom and milk"   "please"

I

I

I

Lover

I

I cleaned her out

I ssssssssssscooped her out he usssssssssssssed me assssssssssss cockk-
kkkkkkkk sssssstretched me long to eat her out I ate her out I ate
her ate ate her her ate her god what a ffffffffffucking feassssssssssst —

//
///!

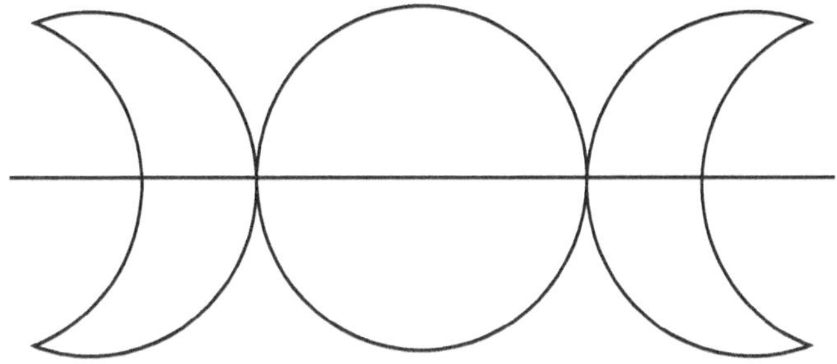

Can you hold this?

No.

Put it to your mouth. It's only water.

Water.

Yes.

As you well know, trauma cannot be revisited by the intellect alone – oh how I loathe the body's emotional procrastinations. Pleased you could proffer me bone broth, a restful slumber in our bed, cool clothes. I remember you read to me in the height of my fever, when I clawed at my flesh and reopened old raised scars. What was it? Something mollifying. Willa Cather, perhaps? The long grasses of her dismal, male prairie? The Nebraska snow? I do recall you read of snow. And you never once begged me to quit this project.

I do not deserve you. I will spend the rest of my days attempting to deserve you.

I woke that ninth morning, naked, on the floor, salt scattered, flesh tender, chalk smudged out. I crawled to the wastebasket on my battered hands and knees, stuck my finger down my throat, and proceeded to throw up everything in my body. I retched for an hour. The things that erupted from my mouth: mucosal membranes, dark and bloody. Something resembling tendons. Curls of hair. Hard knots of flesh. I wept. *I want.* The last bits of bile, the last scraps of arousal, of meal. Then I lifted and turned around and shat into the same wastebasket.

I needed it out of me. Every last, hot, dripping shred. Every last memory of desire for that act of mine. Mine, alone. Undrugged. Sober. Clear-eyed. Oh. All of it, out.

When I was finished, I stumbled to my suitcases, threw on a pair of trousers and an undershirt. Carrying the wastebasket, I opened the door to the hallway. There crouched Eurydice, teeth bared silently, backed against the wall.

"It's done," I said feebly. I held up the wastebasket. "We're done."

I stumbled into the storm room and kicked open the door. Mist lashed at my face: the bay was blanketed with a thick cover of fog, the bodies of starlings dead at its feet.

I retched one more mouthful of bile into the wastebasket, then surged forward into the gray.

Knowing what I knew, our nighttime necromancy meant I couldn't merely dump this waste into the ocean without polluting the whole of it. Near the house, and I'd poison the groundwater. The damp salt spray coated my arms in a sort of rind. The woods were what was left to me; I went into the woods.

The pines murmured. Ghost pipe peeped up through the moss, their small buds still translucent, not yet pink with the knowledge of their sex. After some time, I realized Eurydice was following several paces behind me, maintaining an even heel. When I stopped to clear my sour mouth with water from a tiny creek which ran down to the bay, Eurydice, too, halted her procession, hiding her bulk behind a fern. I held out some water in the cup of my hands. She sat, neither trembling nor cocking her head in interest.

"Fair enough," I said.

At last, we came to The Chasm. Down the center of a mound of exposed marble ran a long and jagged cut, as if some great god had stabbed at the earth with a divine knife. I scrambled up the side, the clicking of Eurydice's nails echoing down the geodic cut. Side by side now, we peered down into the crevasse. Small bits of seashells and petrified wood and apatite studded the cream and rose lines of rock. The darkness seemed unending, though I knew that in this underworld, creatures still thrived – bats and worms and light-averse lichen, an entire ecosystem of darkness dwellers.

I tipped the wastebasket. There was no ceremony. No last words. I emptied the contents of myself, of Anna, of Lyle, all that which had been held within my stomach, into The Chasm. I left the wastebasket behind, and started into the woods once more, Eurydice padding faithfully at my flank.

And then I stayed in that house for nine more days. It's a baffling thing, lover, to remain in a house where one has been quite literally inverted and to then maintain, somehow, a passive participation in quotidian life. Routines remained: we ate breakfast, we read by the fire, I wrote poetry, we spoke some. During that time, Eurydice never left my side, often so underfoot I found myself carrying her around in my arms like a baby.

I could no longer look Anna in the eye, and left the room whenever Lyle arrived. I took many long walks along the beach to avoid them both, as well as to escape the idle prattle of Anna's husband, now so loud in the room as to be unbearable. I'm not sure what she and Lyle did now in the studio, but no more infant creatures died around the house. At least there was this improvement.

I now slept on the couch by the hearth, under the pretense that I was "too cold" to stand the studio. When I awoke, it was to long, red lines running up and down my arms, and I recalled my nails scratching at my skin in the night. How I longed to abandon this traitorous body, this traitorous mind.

One morning I turned over and saw a cardinal perched on the windowsill. I felt emboldened. So much so that when, at supper, Lyle said something asinine about painting – "In my practice, I like to preserve the quality of light held within the room" – I laughed derisively and replied, "Oh Lyle, let's not be ridiculous. We all know your *practice* has nothing to do with light."

"Maxie!" Anna cried. But I was already out the door, Eurydice hot on my heels, savagely triumphant.

"Maxie."

I kept my back to her, my face to the sea. I held Eurydice tighter to my chest and we watched a wave crash against the hard, black edge of the shale jutting out into the water.

Anna appeared and sat down beside me, shifting to get comfortable. We watched the gray tide in silence.

Finally, she looked at me, tendrils of her pale hair sweeping across her cheeks. When I looked back at her, I could see her eyes were filled with tears. Eurydice laid her head upon my shoulder and sighed.

"You hate me," Anna said, the roar of the sea and the wind almost drowning her out. "Don't you?"

I shook my head. "Explain," I said.

I felt her shudder, either from the cold or from silent weeping. I didn't care either way to discover the reason for the movement. A foghorn boomed from the lighthouse in the distance, and Eurydice howled briefly along with it.

"I don't know what to say."

"Find a word," I demanded.

She took a shuddery breath.

"It's just," she began, "you're so *between*, Maxie, darling, it's what I've always loved about you, so *between*, and if anyone could do it, it would be you —"

"You know," I said, "the way you use people up? That inclination you have, that we're all so captivated by you we'll do anything to please you? It isn't charming, Anna. Not even remotely."

"I know," she whispered, so softly I couldn't be sure if it was the sea or her body sighing.

"And what for, even?" I continued, my voice growing harder. "Why were we doing that for you? What was it about? Do you even realize what you put me through? Not just now, but always! Our entire friendship has just been this. This awful, constant *usage*. I can't and I won't any longer." I hadn't realized I was shouting until my words came to their natural finish.

She sobbed, collapsed onto her knees, utterly defenseless. I felt pity burn a path to my chest, but I didn't want to give in just yet. I glared out at the infinite, endless ocean and buried my mouth in Eurydice's fur to stopper my compassion.

It remains a regret of mine, that my hardness won out.

After some time, Anna rose from the rocks. I listened to her feet find their way over the hardened white barnacles, the mussels peeping up through the kelp, the sounds of her body dissolving into the oceanic static. A gull struggled past, crying into the spray. Eurydice shivered in my arms.

That afternoon I packed my suitcases. It pained me to watch Eurydice put herself between me and my belongings, ears down, tail drooped; as if she could keep me from leaving by refusing to let me pack. I patted her head, tried not to cry.

A folded slip of paper slid under my door. *Sweet Maxie please,* in flowery script on the front. I crumpled it up without reading and threw it out the window.

I picked up my suitcases. I left out the back door. I walked the five miles to the bus station. I got a one-way ticket, and I left that place. I did not speak to Anna again.

I heard, from someone I knew under the façade of friendship, that a mere nine months after I left, Anna's body had been found in the heart of the woods, atop The Chasm, snakes streaming from every orifice. But I wasn't to know this until much later. Just after I met you, in fact.

For days I let the bus carry me farther and farther away from Anna, through fits of waking and fits of slumber, my feverish forehead pressing smudges upon the windowpane. Passengers boarded, fidgeted, fiddled, departed; we were wraiths to one another against the flurry of scenery, the lift and dip of the sun and moon. Rest stops in the woods, meals at diners off the dull gray road, furtive sex squatting against my seat while everyone else slept in jumbles. Lips chapping. Skin peeling from my knuckles. My mind tried not to know anything at all. I passed through the country, filling and draining my body.

When, at long last, hills slid into black volcanic mountains, pine trees became sage shrub and cacti, the rivers dried up, and the land lengthened out, I asked the driver to stop. He asked me if I had any luggage, and I shook my head. *Leave it all. Let it go on without me.* The bus trailed off, swirls of dust and heat warping the vision of its shelter.

I found myself on the side of the road, a crop of rock curled like a mule's ear and the setting sun before me. Cacti and the spears of agave rose stark from the dirt, shadows stretching over the shrubbery. Sage cleansed the air. Something somewhere wailed.

The West bore my return gracefully. I tipped my head, and cursed its parched teat.

I stumbled over the earth, soil already cooling. A copse of brambles in the distance meant a spring, and while I shouldn't sleep there for fear of mountain lions, I could freshen up and guzzle some water before the long, cold night I would spend pushed against the mule's ear. Lizards skittered before my clumsy feet. A ground owl hooted. Coyotes yowled in the canyon beyond. Clever creatures clicked, screeched, swooped. Desert dwellers came alive at night; their calls and blooms thickened the air. I quickened my pace until I reached the spring. Lifting my body up, through, thorns thicket surly wilderness, scratched now bleeding, I parted a curtain of horned brambles, mouth thick with the promise of water –

Before me, a rattlesnake. Tongue flickering, tasting my stink. It was curled on a stone in the center of the spring, tail upright. Rattle: the bulbous tip shivered. The moon echoed in the dark and fathomless pool. Slowly, the snake lifted its head into the air.

"//," I said. I hadn't thought of it, but there it was. A peal erupting from within me, crawling from my depths out onto my lips, riding my tongue barebacked, I could not contain it. The language of me spilled into the cool, riotous air.

The snake's tongue stilled mid-flicker. Eyes went glassy. The rattling came to a halt. Still as a sculpture, it could no longer move itself. I understood, in that moment, that I and I alone controlled the serpent. I could make it leave, dance, eat its own tail, feed itself to the hawk circling us from above.

I reached down, took its length in my hands. The scales felt smooth and sly to the touch. Beautiful, diamond-backed, moving in its vulnerability. It deserved to be painted. I held the snake aloft and, with one great and roaring rip, tore the body in two. Blood spattered the leaves, the cacti, my chest, my face, ran down my arms and dribbled off my elbows into the scrub. I flung the severed rattlesnake body into the night. The hawk dove.

Then I bent down, thrust my hands into the water, and drank.

ACKNOWLEDGMENTS

Thank you to the editors of *The Best American Experimental Writing of 2020*, *McSweeney's Quarterly Review*, *Puerto del Sol*, *The Rupture*, *Threadcount*, and *Caketrain*, in which various editions of these deserts first appeared.

To Sam Moss and Andrew J. Wilt at 11:11 – for your belief, care, and enthusiasm, and for liking my lines so much you wanted to put them on a throw pillow.

To Patrick Cottrell, LA Warman, Lillian Paige Walton, Camille Acker, Brian Evenson, Thalia Field, Carole Maso, Olivia Olsen, Oliver Strand, Sarah Rose Etter, Desiree C. Bailey, Chelsea Hogue, Matt Hedley, Ali Gauss, Heather Holmes, Yeji Ham, Rivers Solomon, Aaron Apps, and others – for the energy you gave these pieces. You've taught me all my best instincts. Thanks, too, to all the musicians I know – for the meter of your joy.

To Halyn Erickson, Aspen Webster, Juli Kosgrove, Ken Neustaedter, Oli Warmer, Coyote Shook, Dana Reichman, Andrea Perry, Greg Cerna, Ever, Jasper Campos, Emily Pendrey, Calil Singla, Charlie Neddo, Cass Laminack, Duke Lambert, Hannah Alpert, Olivia Leonard, Alex Reynolds, Jessie Sullivan, Enoch Riese, Maggie Foley, Amy Martin, Ellen Jones, John Brewer, and Elizabeth Brewer – for keeping me alive and fed and laughing and held.

To Asher – I don't love you much, do I? Just more than anything else in this whole world.

Photo Credit: Emily April Allen

—— ABOUT THE AUTHOR ——

Carter St Hogan is a trans nonbinary writer, musician, and educator. Their fictions, essays, and poetry comics have been published with *Best American Experimental Writing, Awst Press, McSweeney's, Puerto del Sol, FANZINE, The Collagist,* and others. S/he holds an MFA in Literary Arts from Brown University. Carter lives in Austin, TX, where s/he performs "homespun blasphemer queergrass" as **Creekbed Carter**, grows okra, and does 8,000 odd jobs for friends. Learn more at cartersainthogan.com.

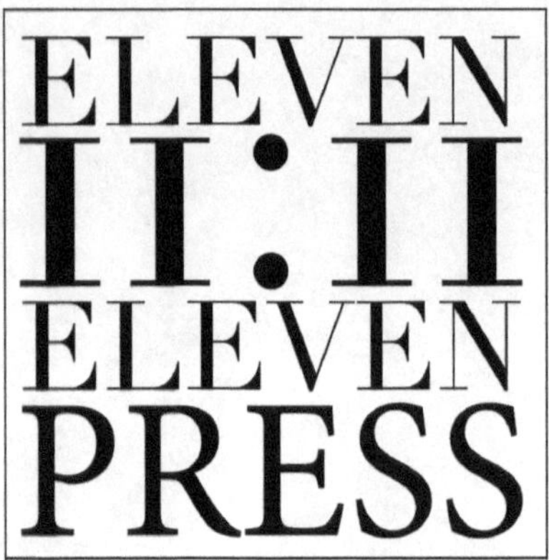

11:11 Press is an American independent literary publisher based in Minneapolis, MN. Founded in 2018, 11:11 publishes innovative literature of all forms and varieties. We believe in the freedom of artistic expression, the realization of creative potential, and the transcendental power of stories.